Did he know who she really was?

Oh, Lord, it had been so long.

His lips touched hers gently, questioningly, and Hillary gave in to her need to sway against him. With a soft sigh she captured his face in her hands.

She felt his moan as Anton pulled her to him and deepened the kiss.

It had been so very, very long, she thought as she came to life beneath his touch. Had she never put him out of her heart? It was as though no time, and yet an eternity, had passed since last he'd held her.

His touch resurrected all the yearnings she had ever felt for him, all the yearnings she had tried so hard to forget.

He released her mouth to kiss her eyes, her cheeks, to bury his face against her throat.

'God, I've missed you, Elaine.''

ABOUT THE AUTHOR

Modean Moon can't remember a time that she didn't want to write; she started a writing club at age eight, wrote her first novel at fourteen. She is now a petroleum landman, writing in her spare time. Modean lives in a restored Victorian farmhouse overlooking the town of Poteau, Oklahoma.

Books by Modean Moon

HARLEQUIN AMERICAN ROMANCE
77—DARE TO DREAM
113—HIDING PLACES

These books may be available at your local bookseller.

Don't miss any of our special offers. Write to us at the following address for information on our newest releases.

Harlequin Reader Service
P.O. Box 52040, Phoenix, AZ 85072-2040
Canadian address: P.O. Box 2800, Postal Station A, 5170 Yonge St., Willowdale, Ont. M2N 6J3

Hiding Places

MODEAN MOON

Harlequin Books

TORONTO • NEW YORK • LONDON
AMSTERDAM • PARIS • SYDNEY • HAMBURG
STOCKHOLM • ATHENS • TOKYO • MILAN

Published August 1985

First printing June 1985

ISBN 0-373-16113-1

Printed in Canada

Chapter One

Anton braked his white pickup to a stop and watched the dust settle in a red haze around him, coloring the truck, covering the already coated vines on each side of the narrow roadway. He was at the northern edge of the vineyard, uphill but still in sight of the grove of trees protecting the two-story Victorian house, which was the only home he had ever known, and of the cluster of newer buildings that housed the winery and covered the cellars.

This was his part of the vineyard. His folly, his family had called it. His downfall, the bankers had hinted. Here he had cleared the virgin hilltop, much as his great-great-grandfather had cleared the first fields, and planted and nurtured the tender hybrids and vinifera.

He stepped from the truck, leaving the door open, and strode into the field. It was August, and the air hung hot and still in the afternoon sun. He lifted a heavy bunch of berries in his hand. For a week now he had been testing the grapes. A day, no more than two, and it would be time to begin harvesting.

He cast a critical glance at the new supporting poles and wires. They were holding up better than he had expected. And the irrigation system installed two years before had more than repaid the initial expenses. And the house—at last he had been able to give it the care it needed. Next year even that work would be finished.

Had that been her voice?

He threw back his head and rubbed the back of his neck with a callused hand, easing the tightness there, remembering the time when he wondered if there would even be a next year. Now there was no question. There would be a next, and a next, and a next. This year's harvest would be the best yet. The last of the notes would be paid. This year's judging at Lancaster would only confirm what at least the eastern winegrowers had known for two years now, that Roeffler's was a name to take note of. And now that his attorneys had finally come through with the necessary permits for him to market his wines outside of Arkansas, the public was beginning to take note, too.

Throaty, probably distracted by something on the other end of the telephone line, she sounded nothing like the voice on the record he had finally located and tortured himself by playing. No. It couldn't have been Rhee. But why, now, was he thinking of her?

He drew his attention back to the vineyard and wondered why he felt no sense of accomplishment in what he had done. After years of never-ending work, success was finally his. But was it really success, he found himself asking, or a prison he had painstakingly built for himself?

Now he knew why he thought of Rhee. Success was meant to be enjoyed. Enjoying meant sharing. And he had no one to share it with. He was thirty-six years old, and alone, as he had always been, except...

He pushed his disturbing thoughts away. Too often, lately, he had remembered. Too often she had crept into his mind, destroying his concentration and clouding his pleasure in the life he had fought so hard to make his. Even now he could see her, her hand tucked confidently in his as they walked through this field, her cheek resting just over his heart as they paused to share a moment of closeness, her mass of red-gold hair flying as she tossed back her head to laugh the husky laugh that always seemed too deep and too rich to have come from her slight body, her green eyes, which sparkled with amusement and darkened with passion.

Damn you, Rhee!

She was out of his life; in all honesty, he admitted, she had probably never been in it. There could be no connection between her and the highly respected music professor who had opened her home to Constance after the end of the summer term so that Constance could attend a concert, a concert Constance had been uncharacteristically vague about. There could be no connection, he insisted to himself, between Rhee Weston, the woman he had learned to love and to hate in a few short weeks, and Dr. Michaels. Dr. *Hillary* Michaels, he remembered.

Swearing, he turned toward his truck. No connection, he thought again. But he wouldn't wait until tomorrow to make sure. He would drive to Oklahoma City this evening, and tonight, after the concert, he'd pick up Constance and meet this Dr. Michaels. He'd smile and be polite when introduced to her, appreciative of her interrupting her staid, matronly life to host a twenty-year old, and then he would finally, *finally*, put Rhee out of his mind.

HILLARY SAT ON THE PATIO, rocking back and forth, rubbing her arms, chilled in the August heat. The scent of roses surrounded her as she concentrated on the hummingbird at a nearby feeder. Her heart was beating as fast as that tiny bird's, she thought.

"What a mess of things I've made," she whispered. "Oh, Lord, what a mess."

She heard the slam of her car door in the drive and Constance's laughter. She braced herself.

Constance burst onto the patio, still laughing softly, so full of anticipation that Hillary hated to say anything, but she knew she must.

"Your brother called."

Constance's smile faded. "Anton? Anton called here? What did he want?" she asked warily.

Hillary straightened in the chair and stretched backward to ease her tense shoulders. "Just to ask that you be ready to leave by noon tomorrow."

She sighed, shaking her head and looking up at Constance. "You didn't tell him the truth about the concert, did you?"

She knew the answer without asking, and Constance's averted gaze only confirmed it.

"No, I didn't," the girl admitted. "Oh, Hillary," she added in a rush of words, "you didn't say anything to him, did you?"

"I should have, Constance, but no, I didn't tell him."

Constance knelt beside Hillary's chair. "Anton *will* understand, afterward," she said. "He won't mind, really he won't, once he realizes how much this means to me. It's just that, Hillary, sometimes he's so straight it scares me, and he's got this hang-up, this really bad hang-up about musicians. But once he sees that I'm serious about this, and that I am good enough to make it, and once he meets Tippy and gets to know him as a person—not as a singer, not as a superstar, but as a real live person—he'll want it for me as much as I want it myself."

"You'd better start getting ready," Hillary prompted gently. "I'll be up in a little while to help you with your makeup."

But Constance remained at her side. "Hillary, I never lied to him. Not really. And neither did you."

Oh, yes, I did, Hillary thought, remembering the pain that hearing his voice that afternoon had brought back all too clearly, *and I still am lying.*

She looked into the girl's clouded gray eyes.

"How do you feel?" she asked, brushing a lock of dark hair from Constance's forehead.

"Scared."

"Good," Hillary told her. "I'd worry if you weren't. It's not every singer who gets to make her professional debut at a Tippy Grey concert in front of fifteen thousand people."

Constance chuckled. "That sounds good, anyway. Even if I am just singing backup vocals and no one in the audience is going to be able to see my face." She caught Hillary's hand in hers. "Thank you," she said, "for everything."

HILLARY LEANED AGAINST A STEEL GIRDER and drank in the backstage activity, knowing that what appeared to be mass confusion was really organized chaos.

She had succumbed to temptation—first by even being backstage, and second by dressing in the dramatic green sheath that set off her eyes, and by allowing her red-gold hair its freedom. She grimaced at the image she knew she had created, one fit for a performance, and then allowed a smile to soften her features. After all, even though she would never again set foot on a stage, she was, tonight, performing.

A Tippy Grey concert was always a major event now, but she knew that this one, a sellout at Oklahoma City's massive Myriad Convention Center, held special importance for her stepbrother. He was secure in his self-image at last, but still this performance had all the earmarks of an "I'll show them" attitude.

Too many people in this sprawling city remembered Tippy as he had been as a teenager—overweight, insecure and belligerent—and too few of them had been able to look beneath the facade he had erected to understand that the insecurity and belligerence came from talent and a deeply sensitive, caring nature.

It was still hard for her to believe that at twenty-four he was firmly entrenched—a legend, some said—as a sex symbol.

The voices from the audience grew distinct now. "We want Tippy. We want Tippy," they chanted, accompanied by rhythmic clapping.

She felt a moist palm slip into her hand and turned. Constance's gray eyes were enormous in the heavy stage makeup.

"Where..." Constance cleared her throat and started over in a small voice. "Where is Tippy?"

Hillary gripped her hand and smiled reassuringly. "Right now he's pacing, pumping up the adrenaline."

"Should I..."

"No," Hillary said softly. "The last thing we want to do right now is break his concentration. How are you doing?"

"Hillary, I think I'm just going to slide right through this concrete floor. I don't know how I'm going to go out on that stage, and if I do get out there I don't know how I'm going to make any kind of music come out of my throat."

"Just remember," Hillary told her softly, "the only people who know who you are are people who know you and love you. You've been through the routines dozens of times, and you've gotten over stage fright before. But—" she eased her hand from the young woman's grasp and reached for the necklace around her own throat "—for a little extra measure of confidence, I want you to wear my talisman."

"Ludwig?" she asked in awe as Hillary fastened the chain bearing the golden caricature of the bust of a mad conductor, wildly waving a baton, around Constance's slender neck.

"Ludwig," Hillary said softly. "Tippy gave him to me years ago for this very same reason."

She took Constance by the shoulders and hugged her. Hillary sensed the tension that heralded the arrival of the band before she heard the noises.

"You'll do great," she said to Constance as she turned her and gave her a gentle push toward the stage.

The voices from the audience muffled and then silenced as Tippy's overture swelled to fill the arena and then erupted into screams of welcome when he made his appearance. He took the microphone from its stand and moved to the front of the stage, each step a sensual promise, as he waited for the cheers to abate, and then the magic that was Tippy Grey in concert took over.

The audience was lost in it, and Hillary was lost in it—hypnotized by his seductive baritone, by the quality in him that made each person think he sang only to an audience of one, by the prisms of light refracted from the iridescent blue of his form-hugging shirt and slacks, by the lyrics, which touched, teased, backed off and returned to touch again.

Hillary tore her attention from Tippy. It was a fantasy he presented, one that she had tried and had found, for her, lacking in substance or meaning each step of the way.

She looked toward Constance and smiled. She showed no signs of her earlier stage fright. Animated and engrossed, Constance in her own special way was lost in the music. A jolt of fear for the younger woman shot through Hillary. She fought it back. For Constance this was right, she told herself. In spite of her family's prejudice.

Hillary leaned back against the girder. "Oh, Anton." She sent the message silently into the night, knowing she would never be able to speak the words to him. "It is right."

But that thought cast a pall over any enjoyment she had felt. She should have told him when he called. She should have at least told him who she was because she knew without a doubt, had there been anything left between them, this added subterfuge would have destroyed it.

But Hillary was a coward. She admitted it and hated the truth that made it so. She had been afraid to defy Jay when he pushed her into a career that was wrong for her. She had been afraid to face him when she admitted that she could no longer live within the restrictions of their marriage. She had been afraid to tell Anton the truth about herself until they had passed the point where the truth could bring anything but pain. She had even been afraid to tell Constance that once, in another lifetime, she had known and loved her brother. Hillary hid any knowledge of her life as Rhee Weston from her students as carefully as she had once hidden herself from the reporters.

So what was she doing backstage at a concert, she asked herself. Was she really giving support to Tippy in this all-important hometown concert? Was she really helping a young girl's career efforts in the face of family prejudice for which she was at least partially responsible? Or was there something more? The thought twisted its way through her subconscious, begging to be heard. Did she really want to be found out? Did she really want to put the fragmented pieces of her life back together? Did she really want, after all this time, to force herself into a confrontation with Anton?

"Ridiculous!" She snapped out the word and then clenched her teeth, hoping no one had heard her. Surely, she told herself, if a confrontation with Anton was what she wanted, she had learned enough in the past four years to admit it and to approach it directly. Surely she had learned enough in those lonely years that she no longer had to hide her feelings, at least not from herself.

The music swelled to a crescendo, and the screams from the arena commanded her attention to the now-dark stage. At the first plaintive notes from the guitar, she closed her eyes. *No!* She should have realized that Tippy would sing that song. "Crazy Blue Eyes" had been one of his biggest hit singles. A solitary spotlight focused on him—shimmering, untouchable, adrift in isolation—as his voice caressed the words she had written, with which she had tried to purge her pain when she first returned. It was a song to Anton, for Anton, telling him of her love, her fears and her loneliness, but he would never know it.

She stared at Tippy, lost in memory, not really seeing him until he stretched forth his arm and Constance glided into the spotlight. "Oh, no," Hillary whispered. "Don't call attention to her. Not tonight."

But there was no escape now. Tippy draped his arm around Constance and drew her close as her clear, resonant voice joined his in the chorus.

As the last poignant notes of the song trembled in the air, Hillary became uncomfortably aware of the presence of someone else. She turned to face the stare of a slim, dark-haired young man only a few feet from her. He seemed innocent enough until she noticed the speculative gleam in his eyes, which seemed to her to scream *reporter*, and fear bordering on panic bubbled through her for just a moment. She caught herself sharply in control and turned casually from him. She warned herself to remain calm as he walked to her and stood with deceptive nonchalance at her side.

"Aren't you Rhee Weston?" he asked.

She heard each word with piercing clarity, even

over the enthusiastic appreciation the audience was giving Tippy and Constance, but did not answer.

"I said," he repeated, "aren't you Rhee Weston?"

Hillary remembered her earlier thoughts. No. She might one day let Rhee emerge, at least partially, from retirement, but not at this moment.

"No," she said. She nodded toward the stage, toward Tippy. "There's your story for tonight. Why are you bothering with ancient history?"

He refused to be deterred. "How does it feel, watching him singing your song to another woman? Is she replacing you, Rhee?"

So, the old rumors still hadn't died. "You have made a mistake," she said firmly, tensing as she prepared to push past him.

He caught her upper arm in his hand. "What forced you out of hiding?"

Hillary looked at him and shook her head. "I said, you've made a mistake. Please let go of me."

She glanced about, looking for a means of escape short of stomping the man's foot or slapping his hateful face, and caught the glance of Jim Wilson, Tippy's road-crew security chief. Quirking her eyebrow and lifting her chin, she summoned him.

He came silently and placed one beefy hand on the reporter's shoulder. "Is something wrong?" he asked.

Hillary smiled at him. "This man has confused me with someone else."

Jim glanced down at the reporter's hand and tightened his hold on the man's shoulder. "I believe you'll let go of the lady, now," he said calmly. "And I'm sorry, but you're in a restricted area. I'm going to have to ask you to return to the other section."

The reporter eyed Hillary shrewdly. "Rhee Weston disappeared off the face of the earth four years ago. Why, tonight, did she suddenly reappear?"

Hillary faced him with a bravado she was far from feeling. "She didn't," she said and pushed past the two of them.

She waited near the exit to the dressing rooms until Jim escorted the reporter to his designated area and joined her.

"Are you all right, Hillary?"

She nodded. "I thought I was tired of hiding," she said, "until he reminded me what it had been like. Thank you, Jim. But I think that I'm more than a little shaken. I suppose there will be more of that if I stay around for the party, won't there?"

"We can keep them away from you."

"And give Tippy a bad press?" She shook her head. "I don't think so." As she fumbled in her purse she admitted silently that she had been looking forward to the party, but she swallowed her disappointment and frustration as she retrieved her car keys.

"Tell Tippy he was wonderful tonight and that I'll call him tomorrow afternoon in Denver, when he's had a chance to get settled in."

Jim only nodded, but Hillary saw the concern and affection in his eyes as she handed him the key ring.

"Give these to Constance, please," she asked. "And tell her that I've gone home, but for her to enjoy herself."

"Do you want one of us to take you?"

"No. No, thanks, Jim. I would appreciate it if someone would get me a taxi, though. And please, try not to let that man find out who I am."

DON'T LET HIM FIND OUT WHO I AM, Hillary thought in the stale and sordid solitude of the backseat of the taxi.

Who was she? Who had she ever been? Not Rhee Weston, surely not. Rhee Weston had been a product of Jay's imagination. But wasn't there a point where she had been, had become, couldn't escape being Rhee? If not, how had she ever been dazzled into marrying Jay?

This is who I am, she thought as the taxi pulled into the drive of her two-story white colonial house. The porch light was on, as was a lamp in the entry hall. She left those as they were and wandered through the darkened house, familiar with the placement of each piece of furniture, each lamp, each picture—each item sought by her, selected by her, positioned by her until she had created a graceful, comfortable and yet, somehow, still slightly formal haven; so far removed from the hectic insanity of her life with Jay

Weston that at times she almost forgot the frenzy of those months.

Only the royalties reminded her, not those from her record—although occasionally, almost as if the public wanted to find out what the old scandal had really been about, there would be a burst of sales—but from her music, the music she had written and had not been allowed to perform; the music Tippy had adapted to his own unique style until she had succumbed to his pleading and had begun writing especially for him.

Was that who she was?

She let herself be drawn into the music room. Or was this the real Hillary Michaels?

She turned on a lamp near the piano, and its soft light pushed the shadows back. A box recently received from her publisher sat near the piano, as yet unpacked. It contained her copies of the last volume of the adult piano course she had developed. Staff paper filled the music rack of the piano. A symphony—*her* symphony.

She slid onto the piano bench and smoothed the pages on the stand. Almost finished now, except for the last movement, tonight it mocked her. It had taken her months to convince herself that it was all right for her to attempt such an ambitious task. Just as it was all right for her to spend a weekend or a week writing a song for Tippy, it was all right for her to take a year to write this for herself.

She began playing the music that had filled her life, but tonight it could not fill her thoughts.

Anton was coming. There was room for nothing else in her mind. Tomorrow at noon he would be here, in her house. Tomorrow at noon she could see him for the first time since she had left him on the side of that small landing strip in Ozark, Arkansas.

She closed her eyes against the memory of how he had looked that last time, as he stood beside her, waiting for Tippy's plane to arrive. His mouth had been set in a grim line beneath the fullness of his mustache. His eyes, which had always reflected, at least toward her, laughter and a joy of living, had been darkened to a midnight storm. Although he stood by her side, he had withdrawn from her. She couldn't reach out to him; she had forfeited that right. He waited until the plane landed, but when she was at last seated inside it and turned to look for him he was gone.

Hillary felt the tears on her cheeks streaming silently downward and recognized the music her hands were playing, her heart was playing—not her symphony but "Crazy Blue Eyes."

How would he look the next day when she faced him, she wondered. *If she faced him.*

True, she believed him when he told her he loved her. True, he had tried to contact her.

No. She wouldn't see him tomorrow. He had probably put her out of his life and his mind long ago. It wouldn't do any good to reopen old wounds now.

She allowed herself to play one more chorus of the song, then closed the cover of the piano and switched off the lamp.

Chapter Two

Hillary awoke to the sound of a blue jay complaining noisily in the tree outside her bedroom. Sunlight dappled through the sheer curtains of the double windows that overlooked her patio. She twisted and stretched, awakening slowly, vaguely remembering that today something would happen. Then she remembered what that something was.

She jerked upright and turned toward the clock. She sagged in relief. She had overslept, but not as badly as she had feared. It was only nine-thirty. While she would have to hurry to get out of the house in time, she could still do it and have a few minutes to talk with Constance before she left.

Hillary pulled on a pair of soft, faded jeans and a short-sleeved T-shirt. Forgoing any shoes for the moment, she went downstairs. While the coffee was being made, she went outside to fish the fat Sunday paper from its habitual place beneath the juniper bushes. She switched off the entry hall lamp and the front porch light, and cast a quick glance toward her car in the driveway to assure herself that Constance had in fact arrived home the night before.

She went back into the kitchen. The article about the concert was easy to find; it filled a quarter of the front page of the entertainment section, complete with a picture of Tippy onstage. It sketched his childhood briefly, mentioning only that he had been born in Oklahoma City and had lived with his widowed mother and attended schools in Capitol Hill until his early teens. The reporter was obviously proud to claim the hometown son and confined most of his remarks to the "electricity," the "brilliance," the "magnetism" of the performance.

Hillary grinned. Either the reporter was a hard-core Tippy Grey fan or no one had ever cautioned him about the use of adjectives.

She saw thankfully that there was no reference to Rhee Weston. Obviously the man she had met was not a local. More thankfully still, she noticed that there was no specific reference to Constance, only to a "compelling and passionate" duet.

She carried paper and coffee out to the patio. She considered awakening Constance but decided to let her sleep for a while longer. It had to have been late when she came in. Hillary had lain awake for hours, it seemed, before finally falling asleep.

Dew still glistened on the dark purple grapes hanging heavily on the fence. She plucked a bunch and carried it to the wrought-iron table.

Constance had chided her gently about having nothing more exotic than Concords, and Hillary had laughed with her. But Concords were exotic enough for breakfast, she thought as she bit into one—or for memories.

She could smell the vineyard in these grapes— the heady mixture of dust and life, and she could feel the coolness of the dim cellars in their juice. It had been a perfect place for healing her body, but more important, her soul. And Anton—Anton had been the perfect guide. At first, fear of discovery had kept her silent; later, fear of eviction. She should have told him; she had known that for weeks. She would have told him, had agonized over how to do just that, until that disastrous newscast had taken all choice from her.

Hillary heard the muted sound of the telephone through the storm door and scrambled to answer it.

The familiar voice was slightly hoarse but still unmistakable. "Hi, there, Big Sis. How's my favorite girl?"

"That depends," Hillary said, laughing. "If you mean your mother, Elaine is fine as far as I know and still in Europe. If you mean me..." She paused; no, there was no need to say anything to him. "If you mean me, I'm...okay, I guess. But if you mean Constance, as I've begun to suspect you do, I can't answer. She's still asleep. What on earth are you doing up this early?"

She heard his short bark of laughter before he answered. "That's wonderful," he said. "She's sound asleep and I haven't been able to sleep at all.'' He hesitated slightly before continuing. ''Did you talk to her any, last night, after the concert?''

''With the hours you keep?'' Hillary asked. ''You've got to be kidding. I didn't even hear her come in. How's Denver?''

''From what I've seen of it—the airport, the limo, and the hotel room—it's just fine,'' he said. ''We're going over in a little while to check out the lights and the sound system. Hillary?''

''Yes, Tippy?''

''Hillary...'' His voice lost its teasing quality. ''Jim told me about last night. Are you all right?''

''Oh. Yes, Tippy. Yes, I am, really. It was just a little uncomfortable, that's all. You, by the way, were wonderful.''

''You think so?'' he asked. ''They did like me. They really did like me.''

Hillary laughed. ''Everybody likes you, Tippy. Don't tell me that's why you've lost sleep.''

''Actually, it isn't,'' he said. ''You didn't talk to Connie?''

''What is this? I just told you I was asleep when she got home.''

''Oooh-kay,'' he said. ''I guess there's no way to ease into this, but I sure wish there was. Connie and I are getting married.''

Hillary felt a wave of dizziness and clutched at the counter. ''Oh, God, Tippy. No.'' Anton—Anton would never approve.

''What's the matter? Hillary, you like Connie!''

''Of course I like Constance,'' she said, ''it's

just that . . . oh, Tippy, her family is never going to accept this. She didn't even tell them what kind of concert it was last night.''

"You mean her brother, don't you?"

When she didn't answer, Tippy continued. "Well, he's going to have to accept it. I've been trying to talk Connie into marrying me for months now, and she's always put me off with 'Anton wouldn't understand. Anton wouldn't approve.' She couldn't upset Anton. I'm afraid it's too late for me to worry about Anton. Connie's going to have my child. She told me he was picking her up today. She's going to tell him today. And then she's catching a plane to Denver tonight to join me. I want you to come with her. We both want you to be at the wedding.''

Hillary swallowed once. She felt her hand sliding on the receiver and gripped it more firmly. Words swirled through her mind, but none paused long enough for her to force them past her throat.

"Hillary." Tippy's voice lowered. "Connie and I love each other. I thought you knew that. I thought surely you must have seen that.''

Now she would have to face him. The thought twisted around her heart as she stared blankly at the yellow daisies on the kitchen wallpaper. She couldn't leave Constance to tell him, alone. Not with that bombshell to drop. Oh, God, she thought, the lies and the deceptions. How they added up. How they compounded each other. How could she face him? She had no idea where his abhorrence of the music industry had begun, but she knew that it was real, and that she had only strengthened it, and now this.

"Hillary? Are you still there?"

"Yes." She could speak. Now.

"Of course I'll come to Denver, Tippy. And yes, of course I do like Constance. And if you're happy, I'm happy for you." She let out a deep breath. "But telling her brother is not going to be easy."

"I know," he said. "I wanted to be with her, but this damned tour has me so tied up I hardly have time to breathe except on a stage or a plane."

"I know," Hillary said, sighing. "I know you'd be here if you could. Don't worry about it, Tippy. Everything will be all right."

"Thanks," he said. "Now do you suppose you could roust the bride-to-be out of her idle slumber and get her to the telephone?"

"I'll do my best." Hillary's chuckle was weak, but she hoped it would satisfy Tippy.

She propped the telephone receiver on the cabinet. *Married? Tippy and Constance married? And Constance—going to have a baby?* She swallowed back a laugh that bordered on hysteria. Her foot slipped on the carpet of the first step. She clutched the banister, a lifeline, as she climbed the stairs.

She tapped lightly on the closed door to Constance's bedroom. When there was no response, she called out Constance's name, twisted the knob, pushed the door open and walked in.

She stopped in confusion. Clothes chosen and

discarded as a result of Constance's indecision as to what to wear the night before littered the bed, but the bed had not been slept in, and there was no sign of Constance. Nor was there any sign of her having returned to the bathroom.

Whirling, Hillary ran down the stairs, calling Constance's name. She was not in the living room, or in the den, or in the music room.

"Constance, where are you?" Hillary called out.

The car was in the drive. Hillary knew that she had to be here, somewhere. Hillary jerked open the front door and raced across the lawn to her car. When she reached it, she saw what she had not noticed earlier—the door, although pushed shut, was not completely closed.

"Constance!"

The car was empty. Hillary sagged against the fender.

What had happened? Where could she be? Unbidden, the thought came to her, *Was this how they felt when I... No!* she told herself as she started back toward the house. This was entirely different. Constance was not missing. Constance was just—

Hillary cried out as something sharp bit into and then slid beneath her bare foot. She bent down and retrieved the object—a ring of keys, hers. She held them in her hand. Constance's house key was attached to it.

"Oh, God," she whispered. "Connie! Connie, where are you?"

Hillary stood there for only seconds, not really expecting an answer but praying there would be one. *Tippy!* She had forgotten all about him. He was still waiting, still expecting to talk to Constance.

She ran back into the house and snatched up the telephone.

"Tippy?" she said breathlessly.

"What is it?" he asked, laughing. "Can't you rouse Sleeping Beauty?"

"Tippy ... I ... she ..."

"What is it, Hillary? What's the matter?"

Hillary took a deep breath and steadied herself. "Tippy—she isn't in her room. I can't find her."

"Maybe she couldn't sleep after all," he said. "Do you think she might have gone for a walk?"

"I don't think she's been in her room all night. The car door wasn't completely closed. I found the keys in the yard. I don't think she ever got in the house."

"My God."

Hillary listened to the silence, not breaking it, not able to break it, until he spoke again. "Call the police. I'll be there as soon as I can."

"No. Wait." She couldn't think right now. "Stay where you are. Let me ... let me call you back in just a minute. Give me your room number and tell them to let the call through."

"You expect me to wait here?" he asked.

Hillary ran her hand through her hair. She had to think. She had to be calm. "Yes, Tippy, I do. I may have to get in touch with you, and I can't do that if you're thirty thousand feet in the air. I'll call you right back. I promise.''

Hillary knew she should call the police immediately. Something must have happened to Constance. She was too levelheaded just to have gone off without saying anything. *Or was she?* Hillary wondered. Was anyone ever so levelheaded that at times... No! Constance was nothing like she had been. The situation was entirely different. She had been so happy last night, and facing her brother couldn't be that frightening. *Her brother.*

Oh, Lord, Hillary remembered, Anton was on his way.

She fumbled through her address book. She had written down Constance's home telephone number, not expecting ever to use it. With a trembling hand, she dialed that number. On the third ring, a vaguely familiar male voice answered, but Hillary was too frantic to stop to identify it.

"This is Hillary Michaels," she said. "I need to get in touch with Mr. Roeffler. Did he leave a number in Oklahoma City where he could be reached this morning?"

"Well, well, if it isn't the songbird," the man said, and then Hillary recognized his voice, but for the moment she didn't question how he knew who she was.

"Bill."

"Right you are, lovely lady."

"Bill, I don't have time to play games. I have to talk to Anton."

"Oh, I'm afraid that's not going to be possible

right now. He's down in the winery, and I don't think he wants to be disturbed. Especially not by someone who wouldn't even return his calls four years ago."

The facts hit her with stunning speed. Bill Roeffler knew who she was. And Anton was in the winery, not on his way to Oklahoma City.

"That took the wind out of your sails, didn't it?" Bill asked.

"I don't understand. Why isn't he on his way to pick up Constance? He's supposed to be here at noon."

"Change of plans, sweetheart. He's already come and gone."

Hillary sagged against the cabinet. "She's there?"

"You've got it."

"Let me talk to her."

"Oh, no. I don't think Anton would like that. And I don't think I have time to call her to the telephone."

Anger washed through Hillary. How dare this man talk to her like this? How dare he? But Bill dared a lot; he always had. And her anger was not entirely directed at him. Most of it belonged to Anton.

"Do you mean he picked her up and took her home and didn't have the decency to tell me that they were leaving?"

Bill's laughter answered her.

"I want to talk to him," she said. "I want to talk to him now."

"Oh, I don't think I can let you do that, either." Bill drawled the words out, letting her hear his amusement.

"Oh, yes, you can, Bill Roeffler." Hillary's anger fed itself, without the assistance Bill was giving it. "Because if you don't, I'm not going to have any choice but to call the police and report Constance missing. I don't believe you. So if Anton doesn't confirm that she is there, I'm afraid that I don't have any other options."

"You'd do it, too, wouldn't you?" he asked.

"Just watch, Bill," she promised. "Just watch."

He let out a quick breath, and Hillary knew she had won this round.

"Hold on. I'll see if I can find him."

Hillary did hold on—to the receiver with one hand, to the counter with the other, and to her temper with the strongest check she could place on it.

It made no sense, she thought. When had he arrived? Why hadn't he even waited for Constance to pack her things?

When at last she heard Anton's voice on the telephone, she barely recognized it. He spoke with an edge of coldness, and yet she sensed an underlying anger as tightly checked as her own.

"Dr. Michaels."

Oh, so very formal and so very distant, she thought and, in spite of that, able to slice through the defenses she had carefully built over the last four years and remind her of all she had lost. She had never thought she would appreciate anything about the years of experience that had taught her to hide herself behind a mask of calmness, but now she did.

"Yes."

"I assure you that my sister is safe."

"Let me talk to her."

"No. Constance is asleep now. And I'm surprised you aren't still asleep yourself. Or are you just getting home?"

"What?" His unexpected attack cut through her facade of composure. "What are you talking about?"

"Except for about an hour," he said, "I was outside your house, waiting for someone to come home, from ten o'clock last night until three o'clock this morning, when my sister arrived—alone."

"And you think . . ."

"It doesn't really matter what I think," he said. "Constance is safe at home now, and I hope that will be the end of the matter."

"Oh, no, it won't," Hillary said, as her anger began once again to assert itself. "Do you have any idea what we've gone through, wondering what happened to her?"

"I apologize for any discomfort I've caused you. Now I believe that *will* be all."

"No, it isn't," Hillary insisted. "I want to talk to Constance. I want to make sure she's all right. I want to know why she left the way she did."

"She left because I asked her to," he said.

"Asked? Or forced? It isn't like Constance to leave like that."

"It isn't like Constance to do a lot of things she's been doing lately," he told her, and she heard his irritation threatening to break through.

She wouldn't argue that point with him. Not now.

"You can't stop me from talking to her."

"Maybe not," he told her. "But I can stop your telephone calls from getting through. She's had all the interference she needs from you."

"Anton..." His name burst from her. She knew why he was acting this way, but that didn't lessen the hurt. "Please! Please let me talk to Constance! Let me hear her say she's all right. Let me hear her say this is what she wants."

"I'm getting ready for harvest," he said. "I've spent too much time on this already. Now, excuse me."

"No!" she cried out. But it was too late. Even as she spoke she heard the decisive click of the telephone being hung up.

She stood holding the telephone receiver in one hand. Her other hand covered her mouth as she breathed in great gasps of air. It was worse, much worse than she had dreamed it could be.

Slowly she replaced the receiver and turned. A spasm of physical pain sliced through her midsection, and she doubled over, giving in to it, but no tears came. She'd have to call Tippy. She'd have to tell him. What? What on earth could she say?

The telephone shrieked at her, and she snatched up the receiver.

"Have you heard anything?" Tippy asked without any preliminaries.

Hillary took a deep breath and straightened upright.

"She's all right. She's at home."

"Let me talk to her."

"No. No, she's at home in Arkansas. I just talked to her brother."

"Why, Hillary? What did she say?"

"He wouldn't let me talk with her."

"What's going on down there?" Tippy demanded.

"I don't know...I..." Then the tears came. "Yes, I do know, Tippy. Oh, God, how he hates me. I'm sorry. I wouldn't have had this happen for the world."

"What do you mean, he hates you? The brother? How could he hate you, Hillary? He doesn't even know you."

"Oh..." She stifled a moan. "He thought he did. A long time ago."

"When—my God. Is he the one? Anton Roeffler?"

A broken sob was the only answer she could give, but Tippy's silence told her that he understood.

When he spoke, he spoke gently. "Why didn't you tell me?"

"I don't know. I don't know why I did half the things I did. It seemed so important to protect him when I first came back, to keep him from being involved in the scandals. I thought if I just broke it off clean with him...there'd been enough hurt already.... And I suppose when I met Constance I...I never really believed that he'd find out, that there would be any reason for him to find out."

"And that's why you were so upset this morning when I told you we're getting married?"

Hillary managed a shaky laugh and wiped at her eyes. "Silly, wasn't it? But none of it really hit home until yesterday afternoon when he telephoned. You'd think I'd learn someday that my actions have a way of coming back to me."

"What actions? My God, you were running for your life."

"No, I wasn't," she said. "Not really. I was just running. Away. Jay wouldn't have hurt me any worse than he already had." She laughed, a short one-syllable sound with no humor in it. "And he couldn't have hurt me as much as he did if I hadn't put up with it. I'm not sure now that I was even running away from Jay. Maybe..." She paused, almost afraid to speak the words. "Maybe it was myself I couldn't face."

"Come off it, Hillary. You've always been the strong one."

"Not really."

"You've always been the strong one," he insisted, "and you've always been too hard on yourself. Anybody with half a brain can see that you're not the type to hurt someone deliberately."

"I don't think it matters whether I did it deliberately or not, Tippy. The fact is, I did hurt him."

"You hurt him," he said, "and then you protected him. Does he have any idea what his life would have been like if you had told the press where you were for that month, if you had told Jay where you were for that month? Would he really have wanted to be dragged into divorce court or had his life history dissected and spread over every scandal sheet in the country? And why, if he cared so much for you, didn't he insist on being with you? God knows I'd never leave Connie to face something like that alone."

"Oh, Tippy. He tried. And I . . . I made sure that he wouldn't."

"God, Hillary." Tippy let out a deep breath. The silence stretched between them. "Are you sure Connie's all right? He wouldn't hurt her?"

"Oh, no. No. He's not the kind. And he loves her too much for that."

"Okay. It's too late to do anything about the performance today. I'll get Mike to cancel the rest of the tour. I'll catch a plane tonight after the show."

"No!"

"What do you mean, no? I'm going after Connie. I can't believe that she's there because that's where she wants to be."

"But Tippy, your career . . ."

"Damn my career."

"She's all right. I know she is. You only have another two weeks. I'll go."

"I can't ask you to do that."

"No. No," she said, "you're not asking." And she knew that this was something that she did have to do. "I feel responsible, Tippy. If she isn't all right, I'll call you immediately. I promise you that. But if she is . . . if she is, the two weeks won't make that much difference."

"Hillary, do you know what you could be walking into down there?"

"There isn't any physical danger," she promised him. "Not for Constance, and not for me. Anton isn't that type. Can't you see? I have to do this. I'm almost thirty years old. It's time I faced the results of my own actions. And I will tell you the truth. Whatever I find, I will tell you the truth."

"I don't like it," he said. "You've been hurt enough."

"I'm not crazy about the idea myself," she admitted, "but I can get there much quicker than you can."

"Damn it, Hillary, I don't want you fighting my battles for me."

"I'm not," she told him. "This one, I'm afraid, is mine."

"Wait. At least let me go with you."

"No." She leaned back against the wall, cradling the receiver with both hands. "You have a performance to give, and I . . ." She thought of the coldness and the hostility in Anton's voice. "Maybe I do, too."

Chapter Three

The sun was behind her, a white glow in the pale-blue sky. The scrubby trees near the highway withstood the sun's heat, but their leaves were lifeless. Hillary had packed some of Constance's things and placed them in the trunk of her car, and she had hastily packed a few things for herself. She had spent more than four hours in the car, more than four hours thinking about what she would face once she reached Anton's home.

Was this trip so very different from the first one, she asked herself. She felt the same sense of hopelessness as she had then. She watched as she sped past the mile markers, knowing that she must soon reach the turnoff and that, even as she watched, she would see the grapes before she reached the exit sign.

That first time... She caught herself thinking back to the events that had led up to it. She thought she had put them behind her, that she would never again let them hurt her. She had been wrong about that, but she had been wrong about so much that this discovery lacked the power to surprise her.

She had been coming from a different direction, lumbering west on Interstate 40 in a battered old Plymouth she had bought with most of her cash after catching a ride into Russellville. When she saw the exit for Clarksville, Arkansas, she realized that after three days of hiding and running, she was within a few miles of where she had started.

Then with startling clarity she recalled the start of her running, the scene with Jay when she had confronted him with her knowledge that the only reason he had married her was to get Tippy's mother's signature on a contract for the under-aged boy. She recalled the awful scene backstage after the concert at College of the Ozarks when he had berated her performance, a performance she had let him shape, a performance she hadn't wanted to give, and she had told him she had never wanted to perform, would never perform again. He had struck her then, knocking her against a chair, and she had fallen. The band had seen it, all of it. But they hadn't seen the scene in the hotel room later, when his words and his blows had been even more vicious.

She had escaped from the room, from him, taking only her tote and his red Maserati, and had fled into the night, stopping only when she ran out of gas and had to abandon the car. She hadn't known where she was, hadn't cared. She knew only that she couldn't go back.

For three days she had been free, but it didn't feel like freedom. She had sent a telegram to Tippy, telling him that she was all right and would contact him later. But she couldn't do that yet, not yet.

She had passed each Clarksville exit with a shudder and continued west. But now her cash was running out. Now she would have to surface. She peeled herself away from the sticky vinyl seat cover, reached behind her and plucked her damp tank top from her back, allowing one fleeting moment of regret for the air-conditioned comfort of the Seville Jay had insisted on providing for her. She gave a strangled little laugh. Maybe she was as lazy and self-indulgent as Jay had insisted she was if the only thing that had penetrated her numbed consciousness was the loss of an air-conditioned automobile.

She tried to concentrate on the gently rolling hills on each side of the four-lane divided highway. It did no good.

It was all waiting for her. She knew that. Just as soon as she could slow down, just as soon as she could be in a space that was truly hers, she'd have to deal with it.

She adjusted the volume of the radio on the old Plymouth and turned her attention to it. Through its scratchy sound she heard the announcer discussing Tippy's newest, a double album, recorded live in concert; concentrating on that was much more soothing than her own troubled thoughts. It was good, by far the best he'd done. His phrasing, almost perfect from the beginning, was even better. There was a new sophistication to his instrumentation. But it was the emotion that he captured, reduced to its essence, and wrapped the listener in, that ensured he'd be making his music for generations yet to come.

Only one cut on this album bothered her, and this was the one now played. "Hey, Rhee, are you listening?" Tippy's voice lowered seductively, barely audible over the cheers of the crowd. "This one's for you." He launched into a plaintively haunting melody, singing to an unnamed woman, telling her that he had finally gotten the house in Malibu, but it was empty, just as she had told him it would be, without love. It sounded to the world like a song for star-crossed lovers, but she knew better. It was his way of telling her that he at last understood her reluctance to let Jay push her into the world of performing, that at last he understood her need for home and stability.

But had her house in Nashville been any less lonely than his in Malibu? Had she ever really had a home? Not with Jay. She knew that now. Not with her father, moving from Air Force base to Air Force base, never staying long enough to make lasting ties, never knowing the closeness of family, barely remembering her mother. No, home had been an illusion that always evaded her, even after Tippy and Elaine had come into her life.

She felt the effects of a sleepless night catching up with her. She consoled herself with the thought that Fort Smith was only another fifty miles down the road. She could stop there. At least she could still afford the air-conditioned anonymity of a motel room. And she could postpone for at least one more day the gently probing questions Elaine was sure to ask.

Without air conditioning the interior of the car became unbearable. Trickles of moisture ran down her back, her legs, her breast, while her palms slid on the steering wheel. She felt her hair matting on her neck and sticking to her shoulders. With one hand she lifted the weight of her hair, twisted it, and held it against her head, but it did no good. Even with the vents open, no air circulated in the old car.

She caught a glimpse of herself in the rearview mirror, wet tendrils of red hair pasted against pale, almost translucent skin now glistening with moisture. Without makeup a dusting of freckles bridged her nose, and dusky shadows ringed her large, widely spaced green eyes. The bruise on her cheek had diffused into a less livid mottling of mauve, green and yellow. As had those on her arms.

She grimaced and dropped her hair. So different from the wigs and makeup of her stage presence.

She glanced at the dash. The gas gauge hovered well below the quarter-tank mark, and she knew that this car guzzled fuel. It would never make it to Fort Smith. And with her dwindling funds, she couldn't afford to abandon another car just because she ran out of gas.

Minutes later she saw a sign announcing an exit a mile up the road. She hesitated when she reached the exit ramp. There was no town in sight. Gritting her teeth, she took the ramp. A small sign pointed the direction to Altus. She'd never heard of it. She shrugged; at least they'd have a gas station.

The road ran beneath the bridge of the interstate highway and then began climbing.

"Grapes?" Hillary asked. In front of her acres of neat rows, acres of staked, heavily laden grapevines stretched across the hill. "In Arkansas?"

She forgot her discomfort in her amazement. And the field was no isolated fluke. As the road climbed the hill and then wound across the top of it, she found herself surrounded by vineyards, but even then the first neatly lettered sign was an additional surprise. As was the second, and the third. Signs advertising Post Wineries, Wiederkehr Wineries, Sax Wineries, Roeffler Wineries. "In Arkansas?" she asked again.

The road twisted around another curve; over the tops of the vineyards and over the tops of distant trees, Hillary saw a substantial stone bell tower.

The town, she thought, and determinedly made her way toward it.

She almost missed the turnoff. Muttering, she slammed on the brakes and skidded to a stop.

There was no town, just a church, sitting in isolated splendor on top of the hill. Between her and the church stretched a well-tended graveyard. Behind the church she could see a cluster of sandstone buildings.

Why here, she wondered. It seemed much too large to serve the no more than dozen houses she had seen since leaving the highway. But drawn to its peaceful stillness, she turned onto the road that ran beside it.

A pickup truck was parked near a building that could have been a school or a large parish hall, but there was no car at the rectory, and not a person in sight.

She pulled to a stop near the bell tower in the shade of a large tree. Inside the car the heat was stifling. Outside a breeze ruffled through a grove of pine trees. She shut off the engine and stepped from the car.

The breeze cooled her immediately. She lifted her shirt away from her skin for a moment and then lifted her hair from her neck, letting the wind tumble it in wild disarray. She wandered through the grove of pine trees, her sneakers scuffling through inches of loose needles, and then, drawn by the sense of timelessness surrounding her, into the cemetery itself.

The gravestones stretched out in neat rows, much as the grapevines had on the hill. There was a continuity to it, she realized as she strolled from row to row. Generation after generation lay buried there. The names on the old stones were the names on the middle stones and on the newer stones: Sax. Post. Wiederkehr. Roeffler. Swiss names. German names. Irish names. Families. A hundred years of living in the same place, of working in the same place, worshiping in the same place, being buried in the same place.

It was a continuity she had never known; a sense of family she had never known.

She lifted her face and stared at the bell tower. What kind of church had these families built, she wondered, generation by generation? It was a massive sandstone structure with strength in its simplicity. Would it be locked? Somehow she didn't think so. She hoped not.

She made her way to the front of the church and paused at the double painted and paneled wooden doors. The knob twisted in her hand. She opened the door and stepped into a world of beauty she had never expected.

She knelt in awe by the first pew and let her gaze wander over the murals with their golden backgrounds, the hand-painted stations of the cross, the marvelous purity of the stained-glass windows, the simple dignity of the magnificent carved altar.

Generations, she thought as she looked at the ceiling made of the elaborate patterned metal popular in the last century. Generations of loving care.

She walked forward to the altar rail, taking in the beauty of the murals and windows as she went, and then turned to look back at the church.

High above her she saw the pipes of a vintage organ.

She closed her eyes and sighed deeply. Music. There had been no time for the healing solace of music, no time in the three days of running and hiding. She told herself she had been gathering strength, but she hadn't. There had been no time for that either—only time for a numb withdrawal from all she had let herself become.

She found the narrow stairs to the organ loft. At the first step she hesitated. She was a stranger here. She shook that thought off. She had been drawn here. She meant no sacrilege. She meant no harm to the church or the organ. She climbed the stairs and stopped at the locked grate that barred her way.

On the other side of the grate the organ sat, keyboard covered, waiting. She studied it from the few feet that separated them and then studied the wooden panels that surrounded the pipes and working mechanism. She smiled bitterly when she saw the handle protruding from the panels. Locked or not, even she couldn't play a hand-pumped organ by herself.

She clenched her hands around the grate and rested her cheek against the coolness of metal as she looked down over the church. Bach. That's what she needed. A Bach fugue, heavy and lifting. Filling this church, filling her. Somber and yet joyous. Repetitious and always different.

In her mind she played. Holding on to the grate, she felt each note, listened until the last one faded away. With a strangled sob she pushed away from the grating and made her way down the winding steps. She knelt once more at the back pew.

Generations, she thought. A century of births, baptisms, marriages and deaths. A century of families needing each other and sharing each other. *But not for me.*

She felt pressure building behind her eyes. "Oh, God," she whispered, "I've got to get out of here before I break down. And I can't do that, not yet."

She whirled and ran from the church. The sunlight blinded her momentarily when she left the dim coolness. She walked with forced slowness toward her car.

She stopped at the car. Where could she go? Not home. She knew she could never return there. Certainly not to her father. He was even more distant since Elaine had finally given up and divorced him, and since Hillary had thwarted his plans for her to go on the concert stage.

She left the car and wandered back into the cemetery, idly, knowing she must make plans and knowing that right at this moment she was incapable of planning. She felt moisture on her cheeks then, and a weariness so great she doubted she could even make it the short distance back to the car. She clutched at the nearest tombstone. And why should she? What could she do when she reached the car? There wasn't anything to leave for. There wasn't anything, right now, to look forward to.

She sank cross-legged onto the grave and felt the pressure of the past two years bearing in on her. Two years of pretending her marriage was working. Two years of trying to be someone she wasn't. Two years of fitting herself into someone else's mold for her until she hardly knew who she was. Two years of feeling more like a defective possession than a woman. She couldn't stop the tears. And why should she do that, either? Here where no one knew her, here where thousands of others had cried, why couldn't she?

"Oh, Jay," she moaned, anger and regret so interwoven she couldn't tell where one faded and the other began, "why did you have to use me? And why didn't I have the nerve to leave you when I first realized what you were like? I'm so angry with you," she whispered, "so angry. And so angry with myself."

A sob broke from her then, and she didn't try to fight it. She leaned forward into the freshly mown grass and gave in to her tears, gave in to the racking sobs that she hoped would bring healing.

Minutes passed before she again became aware of the grass beneath her cheek. Sniffling one last time, she sat up, brushing the moisture from her face.

She saw the long shadow on the grass beside hers at the moment she heard the voice, a deeply masculine one coming from somewhere near her right shoulder.

"Do you need any help?" the voice said.

How long had he been there?

She whirled and found herself staring into the deepest blue eyes she had ever seen.

She fought for composure. "Who..." she whispered, unable to say anything else.

There was concern in the rich timbre of his voice and a questioning of who she was and why she was there, but she swore that for the first moment a flash of something else had sparked in his eyes.

Mesmerized by his eyes, Hillary was lost in the depths of them for seconds and then, confusion clouding her thoughts, she began scrambling up.

"No. That's all right," he said. "I didn't mean to frighten you. I saw you leave the church. I only came to offer my help, not to intrude on your privacy."

"Have you been here long, Mr...."

"Roeffler. Anton Roeffler."

Roeffler. She recognized the name. One of the eternals.

"And no, I haven't." It was as though he sensed her underlying question.

She laughed shakily and brushed her cheeks with her fingertips. Now that she had broken eye contact, she was reluctant to look at him but felt even more ridiculous staring at the tombstone or the ground. She glanced up.

A tentative smile lifted the corner of his lips beneath a full dark mustache. Olive skin, deeply tanned, stretched tautly across well-defined cheekbones and a strong jaw, shadowed by heavy sideburns. Straight, untamed mahogany hair fell almost to his shirt collar, while a shock of it brushed across his wide forehead.

A flash of recognition jolted Hillary, but she fought it. She had never met this man before. She was certain of that.

He wore work clothes—faded, worn jeans and an old blue shirt with the sleeves rolled up, exposing tan, muscular arms.

Hillary shook her head, pretending it was to clear her hair from her face. It had been safer looking at the tombstone.

She sniffed once again, and he handed her a snowy white handkerchief. She noticed his hands. Large, strong. A workman's hands except for the well-cared-for nails.

"This was silly of me," she said, embarrassed by her loss of control and wanting to explain it away to him, and to herself. "I don't know why . . . Yes, I do," she said, sighing, and surprising herself with her honesty.

She waited for his careless prying.

He sat down, crossing his long legs, and plucked a blade of grass, still watching her, almost cautiously it seemed.

"Visitors often come to St. Mary's," he said slowly. "Some are just tourists, curious, looking at the building, but others come for deeper reasons. There seems to be a peace here, a calming influence, a sense of the immortality that's a part of us all."

She wiped her eyes with the handkerchief and blew her nose, no longer embarrassed but feeling strangely comforted by his presence. His words so closely echoed her own thoughts. She glanced up at him. A slow smile softened features that a moment before had seemed almost harsh.

"There's a faucet over there," he told her, "and I have a towel in my truck, if you'd like to use it."

How very nice of him, she thought. First his handkerchief and now a towel, and he hadn't asked her one awkward question.

"I would," she said, feeling her own smile answering his. "Thank you, Mr. Roeffler."

He rose lithely and held his hand down to her. "Anton," he said.

"Anton." She liked the sound of it. It suited him, at least the facet of him she had seen so far. Strong—she could see that. Reliable—that she only sensed. The name that she had used for the past three days came easily to her now, the name of the one person who had ever given her the feeling of home, someone who wouldn't mind her borrowing her name. She reached for his hand. "Elaine Grey."

She should have told him then. She knew that now, four years and so much pain later. But then—oh, it had been so easy to justify it. It was only three days and not much more than thirty miles from that final scene with Jay, and Anton Roeffler had been a stranger to her. Later, after he had helped her find a job, helped her find a place to live, helped her find, within herself, a will to go on, she had already heard his disparaging comments about a group of transient musicians who were playing at the club at the Wiederkehr Winery. She had already learned that he harbored a distrust, but not the reason for that distrust, for anyone connected with the music industry. She had also learned that the fleeting infatuation she had felt for Jay Weston at first had been just that, aided and nurtured by his own manipulative courtship, and was so far removed from what she felt for Anton that there could be no comparison.

And Anton loved her, too. She knew that without having to hear the words. At least he loved the person he thought she was. Elaine Grey, a borrowed name. A schoolteacher, a resurrected profession. On summer vacation without a contract for the coming school year. Bruised by a car wreck. It had been so easy, when she first met him, to tell him those half-truths and lies. And so hard to live with them later. So hard, when he held her close and murmured Elaine's name in her ear. So hard, when her body ached for the fulfillment of his love and he couldn't understand why she pulled away from him. So hard, that she had promised herself that she would tell him the truth.

That night they had gone out to dinner. In the candlelit darkness of the Weinkeller, a restaurant in the original cellars of the Wiederkehr Winery, she tried to say the words. Dancing later, in the lounge across the driveway from the restaurant, she tried to say the words. It was so hard with him holding her, knowing that he might never want to hold her again, that she couldn't utter them. In the darkness of the car, driving back to her room, with his arm about her shoulder, the words lodged in her throat, but she had promised.

"Anton, I need to talk to you about something."

"What is it?" he asked, nuzzling his chin across her hair.

"It isn't easy..."

"What the—" He broke through her words. "I'm sorry. There's a light on at the winery. Do you mind? I need to check that out."

Relieved to be able to avoid her confession, even for a few more minutes, Hillary agreed.

They were silent during the short ride from the highway. He parked several feet from the building.

"The light is in my office," he said. "Wait here."

"No. Let me go with you. I'd feel better if I did."

He nodded. "It's probably nothing."

They entered the building through a side door, into the cellars, and walked through rows of the enormous wine casks to the narrow flight of stairs leading upward.

Light streamed through a partially opened door, and Hillary heard the sound of laughter. Anton motioned to her to stand to one side and pushed open the door.

"Well, hello, cousin."

She recognized Bill's drawl and stepped to Anton's side. Bill sat in Anton's chair with the blond waitress from a restaurant in Ozark draped over his lap. Across the room, a small portable television played soundlessly. A bottle of Roeffler's champagne and two glasses sat on the desk. Two bottles, empty, were pushed to one side.

Anton didn't answer Bill's greeting, and Hillary sensed the anger running through him.

"Well," Bill said, "we were just leaving." He patted the blonde on her jeans-clad hip. "Isn't that right, honey?"

She scrambled from his lap, looking stricken, and Bill stretched up from the chair. He picked up the bottle of champagne, hooked an arm around the blonde's waist, and ambled from the room.

"Have a nice evening," he said and winked lewdly at Hillary.

They listened to receding footsteps, the sound of a distant door being slammed and the roar of a car engine before Hillary saw Anton's tensed muscles relax. He picked up the two empty bottles and the two plastic glasses and tossed them in the wastebasket.

He turned to her with a sheepish grin. "I wish we hadn't walked in on that," he said.

There was nothing she could say, no answer she could give him to ease his disappointment in Bill's actions. He held his hand out to her, and she walked to him, let him draw her to him and fold his arms around her. She listened to the steady beat of his heart beneath her cheek.

"Now, about that talk," he whispered.

Oh, no. Not now. She couldn't do it now.

"Anton, I ..."

"No," he said. "Let me go first. I've been trying for days to find the right time to say this. God knows this certainly isn't it, but I don't know if there ever is a wrong time for what I need to say. I love you, Elaine."

Hillary closed her eyes and fought against crying out, *But I'm not Elaine!*

"I think I've been waiting for you all my life."

His chuckle rippled the chest muscles beneath her cheek.

"Is there ever an original way to say this?" he asked. "I guess not. I don't have a lot to offer you right now. The winery is just breaking even. But in a few years ..." She went tense in his arms, and he pulled her closer. "I can't wait a few years," he said. "I need you with me now. Marry me?" he asked. "We'll have a good life together."

A good life? Oh, yes, she knew it would have been. It was the life she had always wanted.

"Anton, I ..." She pushed away from him, twisting to one side. *Too late! Oh, she had waited much too late!*

"Elaine?"

He reached out to touch her shoulder. She whirled away, and as she did her glance fell on the portable television, fell on it, and locked there on a picture of herself, which cut to a video tape of Jay, flanked by two suited men walking into what she recognized as the courthouse in downtown Nashville, which cut to another tape—one of Tippy, surrounded by the press.

"Oh, God," she whispered.

"What is it?" Anton asked. "What's the matter?"

Numbly she crossed the room to the television and adjusted the volume.

"Of course we haven't given up hope," Tippy was saying. "But it looks grim now. It's totally unlike Rhee to have disappeared like this. I can only hope at this point that the telegram we received was not a ploy, that she did actually send it."

The camera focused on a brunette newscaster. "The search for Rhee Weston's body has been called off in the area north of Clarksville, Arkansas, where her car was located almost a month ago. Authorities in Nashville have declined to comment on the reports that murder charges may be filed against the flamboyant promoter husband of the missing singer."

Hillary groped for a nearby chair.

"What is it?" Anton insisted. "What's wrong?"

Hillary looked up at him, at the concern in his midnight eyes.

Dead. They thought she was dead. And Rhee Weston was. Oh, why had she put it off for so long? She tried to speak and couldn't. She swallowed. Never looking away from his eyes, she whispered the words.

"I'm ... Rhee Weston."

She saw the confusion clouding his eyes, and then the shock.

"You're ... ?"

She felt him withdrawing from her.

"I have to go back," she said. "I never wanted to go back."

He was no more than two feet from her, but she sensed an insurmountable distance between them.

"I tried to tell you. I tried so many times to tell you."

"You'll want to use the telephone."

She took a deep breath and nodded. "Yes."

Woodenly she rose from the chair and crossed the room. Her fingers wouldn't function properly. She tried three times before she managed to dial Tippy's unlisted number in Nashville.

A man's voice answered.

"Let me . . ." She cleared her throat and started over. "Let me talk to Tippy, please."

Of course he would ask who she was. No one got through unless expected.

"Tell him . . ." She thought of the one name he'd believe. "Tell him it's Elaine Grey."

From the corner of her eye, she saw Anton look at her sharply.

Tippy came to the phone immediately. "Mom. What is it? Have you heard anything?"

"Tippy, it's me." Her voice threatened to break. "I just saw the news. I'm all right."

"My God, we've been so worried. Where are you?"

She turned toward Anton. "It doesn't matter," she said. "I . . . I have to come back. Can you send the plane for me?"

"Of course. Now. Right away."

She covered the receiver. "Where is the nearest airport where a small plane could land?"

"Ozark," Anton said emotionlessly.

She didn't want to look away from him, didn't want to say the words that would take her from him, but she knew that she already had.

She moved her hand. "I'll meet the plane at the airport in Ozark, Arkansas," she said. "And Tippy, please don't tell anyone, except your mother. Not just yet. I don't want to be met. I don't think I can face that right now."

"No. No, I won't say anything." He called out to someone in the room. "Hillary, just remember—we love you. Mom and I both love you. We'll be with you."

Her voice broke then. "Thank you," she whispered and hung up the phone.

Anton stood across the room from her. Tippy and Elaine loved her, but she saw no vestige of love in Anton's eyes. A chasm of her own making separated them.

"I really did try to tell you, to explain. . . ."

He stood silently watching her for a moment before he spoke. "I don't think there's any explanation you could make that I would understand. Not now."

And there wasn't. Hillary knew that too, now, as her heavy Buick carried her in air-conditioned comfort toward the turnoff. But couldn't she have tried? Yes, this trip was so different in many ways from the first time, and yet was it, really?

She saw the exit sign and switched on her turn

indicator. She could go on past. She didn't have to stop. Tippy would understand. But she wouldn't, she realized. She pulled into the exit lane and lifted her foot from the accelerator. Grapes. She saw the vines on the hillside, marching upward in neat rows. She pulled to a stop at the stop sign. Straight across the narrow highway, an on ramp led back onto the interstate highway. Tilting her chin, Hillary turned to the right.

Chapter Four

The driveway had been paved. Neat, white fences bordered each side of it. Steeling herself, Hillary turned onto the drive and followed the curving path to its end.

She smiled when she saw the house. Anton had restored it as planned, but she doubted that even when new it had seen the elegance he had managed to achieve. Painted a restful green, with its porches, balconies and trim in cream, the sash picked out in a darker green, it stood proudly beneath the tall oak trees.

She glanced to the right, to the neat cluster of wood and metal buildings that comprised the winery. There had been additions made there.

"Enough!" she said. She was not a tourist. She had a job to do.

She glanced into the rearview mirror to make sure that her hair was still tucked into the stylish knot she wore. Her lipstick was gone. She wished that she had stopped earlier, on the road, but the driveway of Anton Roeffler's house did not seem an appropriate place to repair her makeup. She switched off the ignition, snatched up her purse and stepped from the car.

She had chosen her clothes with special care, knowing that she needed to make an appearance that afternoon, and knowing also that few things in her wardrobe would remain fresh-looking after the five-hour drive. She caught a glimpse of her reflection in the window of her car. The slim skirt and silk blouse had borne up remarkably well and still gave her the appearance of a composure she was far from feeling.

As she stepped onto the shaded front porch, the carved front door with its etched glass center pane swung open. A tall, slender woman in her sixties greeted her.

"I'm sorry," the woman said, smiling pleasantly, "but we don't have tours on Sunday."

Hillary returned the woman's smile. This must be Anton's mother. She saw the beauty he had described so proudly as well as the years of hard work that had left their mark. "I know," she told her. "I'm Hillary Michaels. I'm here to see Constance."

"Oh." A worried frown creased the woman's brow. "Won't you come in, Dr. Michaels?"

She stepped back to allow Hillary into the house and stood just inside the door. "I . . . Will you wait here?" she asked.

Hillary nodded and watched the woman hurry down the hall. So far it had been easy, she thought. Too easy. She glanced about the interior of the hallway, curious. Anton's home. Yes, she thought, he had done a remarkable job on it, from the color selections she could see in the rooms opening onto the hall to the gleaming enamel on the woodwork. She had known he would. She fought back a wave of bittersweet longing.

Another smile tugged at her lips when she saw the framed picture on the table in the entry hall. She walked to it and picked it up. It had been hanging with a cluster of other family pictures on the wall in this hallway before the renovation. She should have known it would still be here. The four young people in the picture stood on the steps of the front porch of this house. Anton, the youngest, he had explained to her so long ago; his brother Ben, now a doctor in Fort Smith; his brother Timothy, now an attorney in Little Rock; and his sister Florence, who had died young, leaving a void in the family that Constance, many years younger than the rest of them, had filled.

Anton stopped at the end of the hall, watching her. He had thought his anger would get him through this meeting. *Hell, he hadn't thought at all!* Unbidden, unwanted, he felt his body's response to her. Why was she here? Her fragile beauty was a lie. Her soft voice was a lie. He must not forget that. And her protestations of concern for Constance... Memory of this latest deception stilled the throbbing ache within him.

There was a coolness about her, a poise he didn't remember. But then, he reminded himself bitterly, he hadn't really known her, had he? *What is it, Hillary,* he wondered. *What game are you playing now?*

Hillary replaced the photograph. She wanted to walk farther into the house to see what other changes had been made but remained where she was until she heard footsteps on the hardwood floor.

She looked up to watch Anton approach. Her heart gave a strange little catch. She wanted to run to him, but of course she couldn't do that. She forced herself to remain still. He seemed taller than she remembered. Before, his height and his strength had been a protective shield against which she leaned. Now—now, she realized, they were just imposing. His hair was shorter, she noticed. The sideburns were gone, but he had kept the mustache. He wore a pale-blue pullover shirt and well-tailored dark slacks. He was still muscular, still trim. And his eyes—his eyes were still the deep, midnight blue she remembered, but now they were devoid of any emotion.

He stopped before her, watching her warily, not smiling.

Anger, she could have understood, almost welcomed, but his silence—his silence spoke eloquently of the distance between them. Obviously, it would be up to her to begin the conversation. Well, if he could mask his emotions so carefully, so could she.

"You knew I'd come."

"Did I? What do you want?"

Hillary shook her head slowly, denying the irony of this situation.

"I want to see Constance. You wouldn't let me talk to her on the telephone."

He remained silent a moment, as though assessing her. Then he nodded once.

"Come with me."

She followed him down the hall to a door on the left. He opened it, stepped inside, waited for her to enter and closed the door.

Still not speaking, he walked to the desk in front of two tall, narrow windows and seated himself behind it.

The room had been converted for his study, Hillary noted. The furniture was large, to accommodate his size, but strictly tailored in a soft ivory to complement the deep blue of the walls and the white trim of the picture rail, baseboards, facings and small mantel.

She stood uncertainly near the door, determined that this time he would speak first. No matter how long she had to stand there.

She concentrated on the view through the windows as she waited, as the seconds stretched into minutes—on the small arbor with climbing roses rambling over it, on the concrete birdbath where a mockingbird perched. Her nerves screamed for him to say something, anything. Instead, she felt his steady inspection.

Why didn't he speak? He was treating her as though she were a stranger. No, that wasn't true, either. She knew that to a stranger he would have been pleasant, if not friendly. He would have been polite, if not open.

"Dr. Michaels," he said coldly.

Hillary whirled toward him but clamped her jaw tightly shut. Still he studied her impassively.

"I think you've made a long trip for no reason. While your show of concern for my sister's welfare is . . . touching, for some reason it just doesn't ring true. If you were truly concerned about her, I doubt that you would have aided her, or fostered her, in plans to deceive her family deliberately. Constance has always been truthful with us. She's an outgoing, sometimes outspoken, girl. It seems completely out of character that we have to find out, by accident, that not only has she been preparing for a career as a professional musician but that for months she has been secretly involved in a relationship she knew we wouldn't approve of."

Where was he? Where was the Anton Roeffler she had first met? Hillary knew that somewhere beneath that cold, emotionless facade, he had to exist. If not, that was the worst wrong of many wrongs.

"So." He rose gracefully from his chair and started around the desk. "You will understand, Dr. Michaels . . ."

"Don't call me that," she whispered. *Not in that voice.*

He stopped in front of her. She saw a bitter twist to his mouth as he spoke softly. "Just what in the hell am I supposed to call you?"

She closed her eyes against the derision in his. At her? At himself?

"Hillary," she said, still whispering.

One corner of his mouth lifted humorlessly. "Hillary."

"Anton, please," she cried out, finding her voice. "Don't take your distrust of me out on your sister. She's a fine young woman. You would have been proud of her last night. She's talented. She's ambitious. This is the life she wants for herself. Please don't confuse what's happening with her with what once happened between us."

"And what did happen between us?" He spoke with deceptive softness. "Hillary."

He wasn't a vindictive man; she knew that. Then why, why was he doing this?

"I tried to tell you I was sorry."

"Sorry? I seem to have forgotten that," he said. "What I remember is that you lied to me. You left my arms and flew to another man. You refused to see me. Refused even to answer my telephone calls. Then you dropped out of sight, and the first sign I've had of you in four years is your necklace around my sister's throat."

"That's how you knew."

"Yes," he said. "That's how I knew. And what was I supposed to think? I spoke with you yesterday. You knew who I was." He stopped, as though refusing to voice his thoughts. "You know how I feel about your life. You've known for years. There's no way I want Constance involved in that."

She felt herself straightening. She had many things to apologize to this man for, but not for her way of life, not as it was now.

"I left that life you hate a long time ago."

"Left it? Really?" he asked. "It seems to me that you're still at least on the edge of it. Constance couldn't have done what she did without your help. She told me that much. Why, Hillary? Knowing how I feel about it, why did you do it?"

The question, she warned herself. Ignore everything but the last question.

"I asked her to tell you the truth about the music."

"Oh, you did?" His composure cracked. Anger reverberated in every word. "Did you also ask her to tell me about her involvement with Tippy Grey?"

"No."

"No. And why not?" he asked.

"Because I didn't know about it! Not until this morning. I thought they were just friends, two young people with a lot in common."

His glance raked over her. "No, I don't suppose you did. You wouldn't have encouraged that, would you?"

She stiffened. Her body ached as though he'd struck her. He had believed all the lies, all the rumors. *And why shouldn't he have?* The thought whispered through her mind. She had done nothing to convince him otherwise.

She thought she had defended herself for the last time, but apparently she hadn't.

"All right," she said. "Let's drag it all up. Let's get it out in the open and look at it. Maybe then we can get to what's really important now."

"No. We won't do that. The time for confessions is long past."

"Yes. Now. I lied to you. I didn't tell you I was married. But I never used you. I fell in love with the life here, with the tradition, with the sense of family, with the continuity of generation after generation. I fell in love with you, Anton."

"Don't—"

"No, I will. I was trying that night to tell you who I was. I knew I had waited too long, but I was going to do it. Maybe if I had, the shock wouldn't have been as great. No, I wouldn't see you. I wouldn't answer your calls. You know what my life was like when I went back. But as for the rest of it—they were lies. All lies. Vicious, vindictive accusations from a vicious, vindictive man. That's why I left him in the first place. I never had an affair with Tippy Grey. My God, Tippy is like my little brother. But I wouldn't tell them where I was. And with nothing else to speculate on, they turned to Jay's stories. It was not a plan cooked up by Tippy and me to pressure Jay into releasing him from his contract. There was no need for that. The contract only had a few more months to run anyway. And since you so obviously kept up with the accusations, you ought to know that none of them was ever proven."

She stopped, breathless. Had she reached him? She couldn't tell.

"Only because Jay died," he said.

No. She sighed deeply and turned from him. She hadn't reached him.

"Only because Jay ... Oh, what's the use?" she cried. "Jay died because he was drunk and high and totally incapable of driving that powerful car. There are many things I am responsible for," she said. "One of them is not telling you the truth. I refuse to take the blame or responsibility for Jay's death. How many times do I have to say I'm sorry? I don't know any other way to say it. You knew me then. Did you really think I was the kind of woman who would do the things they said I did?"

He turned from her and faced out the window. "No, I didn't. But then, I thought you were Elaine Grey. A schoolteacher on summer vacation. No, I didn't think you capable of lying. I trusted you. I loved you. I wanted to protect you. I wanted to make you my wife."

He walked to the window and pulled back the sheer curtain, still looking outside. "How you must have laughed at my clumsy proposal."

"Anton, please." A sob broke from her.

He didn't turn. The silence stretched between them.

She felt the pressure building behind her eyes and catching in her throat. She fought it, fought to remain calm.

"Please," she repeated. "Just let me see Constance. Then I'll leave. I'll get out of your life. I'll never bother you again."

"Will you?" he asked. "I wish to God that were possible."

He dropped the curtain and turned abruptly.

"All right," he said. "You can talk to her."

HILLARY WAITED in a deep wing-backed chair near the small, cold fireplace. With Anton no longer there to watch her, she gave in to her need to huddle into herself, but she would not give in to her need to cry. She had cried enough over her past, and she had already paid enough for her mistakes.

For not quite two years she had been courted by, wed to or manipulated by Jay Weston. It had colored her entire life, but she refused to let it negate the person she knew she was.

Each step in the past four years had seemed a major victory—facing her father's disappointment in her; completing her graduate work; interviewing for her present position, knowing that she had the interview only because Elaine had called old favors from the president of the university; winning the job on her own merits.

She had built a good life for herself, step by painful step, and while she admitted she owed Anton more than she could ever repay, she would not let this step destroy the work of all the others.

She turned as she heard the door opening and stood as Constance rushed across the room to her.

"Hillary!"

The young woman threw her arms around her,

enveloping her in a hug that threatened to push her backward. She sensed the desperation in Constance's actions and held her close.

"We were so worried about you. Are you all right?"

"Yes. Yes," Constance said. "I didn't mean to worry you. It was just such a surprise finding Anton there, in the middle of the night, and he demanded that I come home with him. Hillary, I thought I could explain during drive on the way back, but I've never seen him so angry."

"It's all right," Hillary told her. "I understand. Really I do. And so does Tippy."

"How is he? I've got to get...I..."

"Ssh." Hillary patted the young woman's back and stepped away from her.

"But I've got to get on that plane," Constance said. "If I can just get to Fort Smith, I can catch a connecting flight."

"And go where?"

Both women turned. Anton stood in the doorway, his mother beside him. The expression on his face was furious; that on his mother's, frightened.

How much had Constance told her family? Not enough, Hillary realized. But how could she tell them any more?

Constance faced them proudly. "Denver," she said. Only Hillary saw the young woman's hands clench. "Tippy and I are getting married."

Mrs. Roeffler moaned and leaned against Anton. He held protective arms around her.

"Is that why you're here?" he asked. "To take her with you?"

He turned his attention to his sister. "How anxious is this man to marry you," he asked, "if he sends a woman for you? If he doesn't even bother to come himself? Where is he?"

Hillary saw the shocked tears welling in Constance's eyes and felt the words as though they were directed at her.

"Stop it!" she cried. "Can't you see what you're doing to her?"

"I'm trying to make her see the truth."

"You're trying to make her see your version of the truth, not what it really is."

She took Constance by the shoulders. "Tippy wanted to come," she told her. "He was going to cancel the rest of the tour. I talked him out of it. Constance, it's only another two weeks. He loves you," she said softly. "He'll come for you now if that's what you really want."

"In the middle of the tour?" Constance asked. "He'd cancel it for me?"

"Of course he would. It was all I could do to keep him in Denver this morning before we found out where you were. But if you can wait just two more weeks, he'll be here, without having to jeopardize what he's worked so hard to build."

She turned to the other two people. "He'll meet your family. He'll stand inspection."

"But..." Constance started to speak.

Hillary, afraid of what she would say, interrupted her. "The time won't make that much difference."

She saw understanding flash in Constance's eyes. Hillary felt her grasp her hand as she faced her brother and her mother.

"All right," she said defiantly. "But you'll see."

She clutched Hillary's hand.

"And even if you don't..."

Hillary returned the pressure of her hand, urging her to silence. Enough had already been said.

Constance turned to her. "You'll stay with me? Please?"

Hillary heard the desperation in her voice and shrank from it. How could she do that? The few minutes she had spent in this house had seemed a lifetime. How could Constance expect her to spend two weeks here? But then, Constance didn't know.

"I...can't—" Hillary began.

"Dr. Michaels obviously has other things to do, Constance," Anton said abruptly. "Of course she can't spend two weeks here."

"Hillary? Please?"

"I can't, Constance."

"Then I won't, either," Constance said.

"Constance!" her mother cried out.

"No! I won't listen to the two of you for two weeks telling me how wrong I am. I won't listen to the two of you telling me what a bad person Tippy is because he isn't here. Because it isn't true. Hillary, I thought you understood! With you here, they'd have to be careful about what they said.

With you here, I'd have somebody who knows he loves me. I need that."

"Two weeks, Connie," Hillary whispered. "It isn't that long."

"No, it isn't," Constance said. "But it can be a lifetime."

"Dr. Michaels can't stay, Constance," Anton said.

"Well, if she can't, neither can I," Constance told him. "I'll leave. If I have to, I'll run away."

"No!" Hillary and Anton spoke as one.

Sobs broke from Mrs. Roeffler. "Please, Anton," she murmured. "Do something. For God's sake, do something."

Hillary felt herself trapped in his eyes, as trapped as she was in the undercurrents swirling through the room.

"Obviously I can't keep you here against your will," he said to Constance, "although at this minute I wish I could lock you in your room. You don't have to run away from us. We love you. We have only your best interests at heart. We don't want you hurt."

"You say you don't, Anton," Constance said, "but knowing how little you trust my judgment, knowing how you've judged someone I love without even having met him, hurts."

"Two weeks isn't an eternity," he said. "If your love can't stand that separation, it must not be very strong."

"See!" Constance cried. "You're doing it already!"

She turned to Hillary with her mouth trembling and tears pooling in her eyes. "Take me with you now," she begged, throwing herself against Hillary.

Hillary looked over her head, to the icy glare in Anton's eyes, to the stricken figure of his mother huddling against him. He loved this girl. She'd known that since shortly after she met him— loved her and was proud of her. To lose her now would break his heart.

But Tippy loved her, too.

She saw Mrs. Roeffler reach out her arms. "Constance!" the woman cried.

Constance broke into sobs and huddled closer to Hillary.

Anton reached for his mother.

His face was bleak when he spoke. "If you really care for her," he said, "you won't let her leave this way."

Gently, he turned his mother and urged her from the room, closing the door behind them.

Constance's sobs grew more violent as she clung to Hillary.

It was almost more than she could bear, being torn between the conflicting desires of the only two men she had ever loved. *Unfair,* Hillary thought. She was caught between the rash, un-thinking act of one and the blind, close-minded prejudice of the other. She captured that traitor-ous thought and subdued it. There was one fact she needed to remember, one fact that bound the two together, and at that moment she wished that she had never met Anton Roeffler. Without her, the two men might have met each other, known each other, liked each other.

And there was more than just their desires to consider; there was Constance, who still sobbed in her arms, and the baby she carried.

Hillary smoothed Constance's hair.

"Ssh," she whispered. "Ssh. You'll make yourself sick. Come on now; it's not that bad."

Carefully, she calmed the girl. "You're not being deserted, Constance. Come on. Let's sit down over here."

As obedient as the child she had so recently been, Constance let Hillary lead her to the couch and seat her.

She took one of Constance's hands and held it tightly.

"You haven't told him about the baby, have you?"

Constance jerked her head up. "I didn't know you knew."

Hillary smiled at her. "Only since this morning."

"I couldn't!" Constance said. "I've never seen Anton like this. I don't know what he'd do if he found out about the baby. I want him to like Tippy. I want him to—" She broke into sobs again and buried her face in her hands.

Hillary reached ineffectually for her but let her hand drop.

"Don't leave me, Hillary. Please don't leave me here alone."

"But you won't be alone, Constance. You have your mother. You have your brother. And in two weeks you'll have Tippy. Surely at that time you can work things out."

Constance turned from her, burying her face against the back of the sofa, crying soundlessly.

"All right," Hillary whispered. Trapped. She was trapped, and there was no escape. "I'll stay."

Chapter Five

Anton stood in the doorway, the huge double doors slid open now, awaiting a new delivery of grapes. The noises of machinery, the shouts and laughter of the workers behind him, faded in obscurity as he watched the two women walking.

Constance's tall, dark beauty was in direct contrast to Hillary's petite fairness.

For three days he had avoided her. Their few words had been limited to stilted, polite greetings when they accidentally met. But his thoughts had never been far from her, and he had found himself watching for glimpses of her—in the tasting room, where she insisted on helping Constance; on the few occasions she had come into the processing room with a message for his mother; evenings, when she sat on the porch swing talking with Constance; at odd moments like now.

There could be no love without trust. He knew that. And she had effectively destroyed that trust years before. So why was he still drawn to her?

He saw Constance stumble and Hillary reach

out to steady her, and he heard the distant sound of their laughter as it floated back to him. He felt himself smile bitterly. He'd not even seen Constance smile since she came home. Nor, for that matter, had he seen Hillary smile. But Hillary, where he and his mother had failed, had the ability to coax laughter from Constance, and he knew, and was powerless to do anything about it without saying things that might forever alienate Constance from her family, that Hillary was seducing the younger woman's affections, just as she had seduced his so long ago.

Be careful, Constance. Don't trust her too much. Don't believe in her too much, he thought silently. But he knew how easy it was to trust Hillary, who could look at you with such innocence in her green eyes, who could smile tremulously and make a man want to protect her from everything and everyone else in the world. He had fallen all too easily under her spell.

Damning himself for a fool, he gave in and let himself remember the first time he met her. He had been loading tools into the back of his pickup truck, glad that his morning's volunteer work of clearing the overgrown yard behind the school was finished, when he saw her run from the church.

He had watched her pause just outside the archway. Sunlight refracted into a red-and-gold halo around her tousled shoulder-length hair. Smiling, he leaned back against the truck, enjoying the beauty of the picture she made standing in front of the sandstone church.

She was upset; he could tell that by her tightly controlled walk and the way she fumbled with her car keys. When he recognized that, his smile faded. He briefly considered approaching her, but an inbred reserve kept him from doing that. She wouldn't appreciate a stranger who could only pretend his intentions were —

His musing broke off as he saw her slam the car door and stumble into the graveyard. His easy long-legged stride carried him toward her before he formulated what he would say. It shouldn't be too difficult, he argued with himself. He'd just offer to help her. That was all he was going to do, he told himself — just offer to help her.

She was deep into the cemetery by the time he reached its edge. He was still some distance away when he saw her clutch at a tombstone, and then crumple beside it.

He paused, watching but too far away to hear, as she gave way to grief.

Grief was a private thing to Anton, and here of all places he felt that it should be respected. He started to turn away, but something about her held him. She looked so defenseless, broken and alone. And God knew he was familiar enough with being alone.

He walked closer, knowing she was unaware of him, and knelt beside her. *Gently,* he warned himself. He saw her steadying, bringing herself under control. *Treat her gently. Don't frighten her.*

He tried for a lightness in his voice that he knew he had not quite carried off when she whirled to face him. God, she was beautiful, even more beautiful than she had seemed on the church steps—even with her eyes red-rimmed and swollen from crying. Even with what he had not seen from a distance—the ugly discoloration of a bruise against the translucent fragility of her cheek and others on her arms. What had done that to her, he wondered with a flash of anger. Then he looked into her eyes. What had put those haunted shadows in their emerald depths? What would it take to erase them? And what would it take to bring a smile to her trembling mouth?

"Hey, Anton!"

Anton felt the rude push of a fist against his shoulder. He glanced to his left. Bill stood there, with tufts of black curly hair sticking out from under the baseball cap he wore as protection from the sun. Bill had apparently followed the direction of his glance and was now watching the two women.

"Fine-looking female," Bill said around the toothpick clenched in his teeth. "Looks like a lady, and yet..." He let the words fade off. "If she was staying under my roof I'd be hard pressed not to take advantage of what she's got to offer."

Anton fought back an urge to wipe Bill's leer from his mouth and from his eyes with a well-placed fist.

"She's not under your roof," he said tightly. "And you'll keep your hands and your thoughts to yourself. What did you want to see me about?"

Bill grinned and plucked the toothpick from his mouth. "Grapes, cousin," he said.

Only then did Anton notice the tractor with the full trailer behind it that had pulled up to the doorway.

"Grapes," Bill repeated, still grinning. "Isn't that what this harvest is all about?"

HILLARY SAT ON THE PORCH SWING, lost in the violet shadows of late dusk, just before dark. Constance was inside, on the telephone, talking to Tippy. They had at least won that concession.

She sighed, tucked her feet under her, and leaned back in the crook of the swing. It was not as cool as it would be later, in the depths of the night, but she enjoyed the soft breeze against her face, and she enjoyed the night noises—the crickets, the plaintive cry of a whippoorwill somewhere on the hillside, the few scattered calls of bobwhite quail, lessening now in frequency but still to be heard, mingled with the periodic sounds coming from the winery.

There was still a cluster of pickup trucks and cars parked there. She knew from the days past that soon the last of the workers would be leaving, all but Anton, who stayed late into the night.

Was it necessary for him to do that? Or was he avoiding her? Either explanation was believable, but she hoped she was not the reason why he delayed supper and sleep.

She heard the front door open and looked toward it. In the fall of light from inside the house she saw Anton's mother standing on the porch. Hillary straightened in the swing as the woman approached her and stopped, hesitantly, it seemed, only a few feet away.

What was this all about? Everyone but Constance had treated her almost as a pariah since the moment she arrived. Could this be an overture of friendliness? She doubted it, but she smiled pleasantly and gestured toward the swing.

"Won't you sit down? It's beautiful out here this evening."

In the shadows she made out the barest lift of a smile on Mrs. Roeffler's face as she seated herself on the swing.

Not speaking, they sat together. The soft creaking of the swing added its sounds to the night noises.

"I want to thank you," Mrs. Roeffler said finally.

Hillary turned to her in surprise.

"For not taking Constance away with you," the woman said. "For staying here with her. For helping her to laugh again. I know this has to have been an inconvenience for you, staying here this length of time."

Hillary shook her head. "I care for Constance," she said.

"Yes," Mrs. Roeffler said, "I think you really do."

"And as far as it being an inconvenience I..." Hillary paused. She could hardly tell Anton's mother how awkward it was for her. "Actually," she said, changing the direction of her thoughts, "the only inconvenience is the lack of clothing I have with me. I need to do some laundry tomorrow, if that would be all right."

"Of course." The woman leaned back in the swing. "I hope you won't mind—there isn't much—everyone in the family is tall, but I found some things of my granddaughter Carla's, Timothy's oldest, that might fit you. I put them in your room. I don't have time now for a shopping trip into Fort Smith, but if you'd like we can take a couple of hours in the morning and go into Ozark and pick up anything else you need."

Hillary felt the glow of gratitude easing through her. Oh, it was more than just an overture. She smiled warmly.

"I'd like that very much. Thank you, Mrs. Roeffler."

The woman touched Hillary's shoulder as she stood. "Inez," she said. "Please call me Inez."

ANTON WORKED AT THE TENSION in the back of his neck with one hand as he stretched and tried to ease the tiredness from his body. God, he was tired. Less than a week into harvest and he felt as though it had been a month.

There was some grumbling among the workers; there always was. It was Friday night. Most of them wanted to get off work a little early. He understood it, but he could do nothing about it. The grapes were no respecters of calendar or clock. At this time of the year, *they* dictated one's actions, not personal desires.

But it wasn't the harvest that deprived him of his sleep; he knew that. It was Hillary, alone at night in a bed only three doors away from his. It was the subtle trace of her perfume that lingered in a room after she left, reminding him of the presence he tried so hard to avoid. It was the bitter taste of betrayal that rose in him each time he remembered their last night together. And yet, her actions now were so like those of the woman he had learned to love. It would be so easy—and disastrous—for him to forget what he had learned about her.

"Well, that's it," Bill said as he approached, wiping his hands on a paper towel, which he tossed carelessly to the floor.

Anton glanced up. "What do you mean, that's it?"

"That's the last of my grapes," Bill said. "Looks like I'm free. Are you going to need me to help around here any next week?"

"There's room for you, Bill, if you don't have things at your own place to keep you busy."

Bill grinned. "Gramps should have realized when he had a good thing going."

Anton knew that Bill referred to their grandfathers, feuding brothers who had divided the Roeffler land. Their vineyards and their wineries had existed side by side through the generations, until this one. Anton had taken over his winery with little more than Bill had at the time he inherited his. Bill was right about one thing. The land should never have been divided. His never would be, if he had any control over it. And what a poor end to half the Roeffler land if Bill was through with his harvest after less than a week.

Bill stood beside him, watching the activity around them.

"I saw Constance in the tasting room today," he said. "She's sure turned into a beauty. She's got a glow about her I've never seen before."

"No," Anton said. Only the one word.

Bill grinned sheepishly. "Oh, well," he said, hooking his hands into the hip pockets of his jeans. "I guess I'd better be getting on. Hot date tonight."

When Anton didn't respond, Bill freed one hand and pushed his cap forward. "You remember Susie Jackson, don't you? The girl from Booneville who's been coming to church up here, making calves' eyes at you for the last month or two?"

"Good night, Bill," Anton said. "If you want to work tomorrow, be here at seven in the morning."

"Sure, cousin," Bill drawled as he ambled toward the doorway. "By the way, I left something on your desk. I picked it up in town at lunch today. Thought you might be interested."

HILLARY LAY SLEEPLESS, watching the moonlit shadows moving across the wall. From a distance she heard the faint hum of the attic fan, which pulled the cool night air into the house.

Sleeping with the windows open was a luxury she had been denied for too long, and yet she didn't sleep.

The winery was silent and dark; she could see that from her window. The house was silent and dark; she could see that through the open transom above her bedroom door.

This was her sixth night under Anton's roof. The sixth night of lying sleepless until the early-morning hours. The sixth night of knowing that had she been honest, or things different, this could have been her home. That instead of lying alone here, she could have been in that other corner bedroom, the one she had only glimpsed the day she had helped Mrs. Roeffler change linens. That she could have been loved and protected, cherished instead of distrusted and avoided.

She tossed restlessly, throwing back the sheet and urging the night breeze to cool her, to soothe her, but no matter how she turned to get comfortable, the feather pillow seemed like lead beneath her head, her cotton nightgown tangled in her legs and its narrow straps cut into her shoulders.

She thought she'd put him out of her mind, her heart and her life. Sure she had, she admitted as she gave a frustrated punch to the pillow. That did no good, either. Groaning in defeat she sat up and swung her legs over the edge of the bed.

Maybe a walk would help. Surely no one would

mind if she left the house quietly. And maybe a cup of hot tea. She was fooling herself, she knew. Her body cried with exhaustion. But maybe the night air, the solitude and the luxury of being able to wander undisturbed in the moonlight would help.

She pulled the nightgown over her head and slipped into jeans, a T-shirt and sandals. She raked her fingers through her hair and grimaced. How much grooming would she need for the trees and the stars?

The back stairs were closer and therefore quieter. She made her way down them in the dark. A sliver of light glowed from under the kitchen door. She paused when she reached it and listened, but there was no noise from the kitchen. She wondered if the light had been left on accidentally.

Hillary pushed the door open and stepped inside, then stopped in shock and embarrassment. Anton sat at the kitchen table. Papers were scattered around him, and there was a plate with the remnants of a sandwich and a cup of coffee in front of him. He rested one elbow on the table as he massaged his forehead with his fingers. He looked up, the expression on his face as shocked as she felt. She read exhaustion in his every feature.

"I'm sorry," Hillary said as she began backing from the room. "I didn't mean to disturb you. I'll—"

"No, wait. Don't go. Not because of me."

She hovered indecisively near the door. Part of her screamed for her to run from the room, yet louder was the urging for her to stay, to be near him.

Somewhere he had shed his mask of cold indifference. He looked troubled, and incredibly weary.

"I...couldn't sleep," she said.

He smiled, a wan imitation of the smile she remembered. "Maybe it's a virus going around," he said. "I can't, either. There's some coffee on the stove if you want a cup."

She nodded acceptance of the unexpected invitation but felt very much the intruder as she took a cup from the glass-fronted cabinet and poured herself coffee.

He cleared a space at the round oak table for her, and she sat down, awkwardly nursing the cup with both hands.

He didn't seem inclined to speak, not even to look at her. Nor was he really paying any attention to the papers in front of him.

There seemed nothing to say. What could she say?

She glanced about the room, remembering the shell of it as it had been, contrasting that memory with the warm, efficient homey place it had become. Across from her, against a brick wall, sat a beautifully restored cast-iron stove. She smiled at the unbidden memory. The stove had been the source of their one argument. He had wanted to modernize the kitchen thoroughly; she had argued for a kitchen very much as he had made it, telling him he should keep the stove, not as an appliance to be used daily but as an accent, a source of heat, a focal point to gather around. At some point the argument had dissolved into gales of laughter, and he had promised to keep the stove if she would learn to bake bread in it.

Her smile turned bittersweet.

"I'm glad you kept it," she said.

She turned to him and found him studying her.

"You were right about it," he admitted. "It made this room more than just a place in which to cook and eat. We spend a lot of time in here in the winter."

"Everything you've done, you've done well," she told him. "You've turned this into a beautiful home."

She saw the quirk of his lip beneath his mustache and the hollowness in his eyes.

"Hillary?"

She watched him as his gaze seemed to examine each of her features—her tousled hair, her face bare of makeup—and she waited for him to continue.

"Hillary? Bill brought me something today. He found it in town."

She felt her muscles tightening, readying for defense.

Anton bent over and retrieved something from the floor beside him. She recognized what it was, but not which one it was, from the size of it. And did it matter which one? It was a tabloid newspaper. Whatever scrap of gossip one had picked up, the others would gnaw on soon enough.

She looked into his eyes, not at the paper, as he straightened. There were questions in his eyes—not, she realized, accusations, but questions.

With hands that refused not to tremble, she took the newspaper. She didn't want to read it; she never read them, but unless she read this one she wouldn't know what the questions were in Anton's eyes.

She opened the folded paper with a sense of inevitability. The front page. She kept hoping that one day her pain and her mistakes would be of so little consequence to the rest of the world . . . She shook her head in defeat.

There were two pictures. One of her, an old one. She remembered when it was made. She had argued then that it was wrong for her, but there it was. The full red wig would have overshadowed her features had she not been so heavily made up.

No wonder Anton had stared at her. What a contrast she must seem now, with her hair falling carelessly down her back and her face scrubbed clean.

And the other picture? She did have to look at it. She did have to acknowledge it. She felt a flash of anger at the invasion of her privacy. They had wasted no time. It was a shot of her house, taken from inside the backyard, showing the brick patio, the birdbath, the hummingbird feeder, the grapes on the fence—even the Sunday paper she had forgotten and left outside.

She glanced at the story. It raked up all the old rumors. She recognized the insinuations of the reporter at the concert.

There was only one thing in the entire story to be grateful for. Hot on her trail, the reporter had neglected his research on Constance, apparently thinking she would be on tour and available for his own special brand of muckraking at a later date. He had grabbed at the name Connie Roff, the one Constance had decided upon as a stage name.

Hillary dropped the paper into her lap and leaned against the high ladder back of the chair.

Inevitable. It had been from the beginning. She had been fooling herself by thinking she wouldn't be discovered. How long would she have to go on paying for those two years?

Anton spoke softly, but some emotion she couldn't identify deepened his voice. "How much of that is . . . true?"

She turned her head only far enough to be able to see his face. Yes. The questions were still there. And they were still questions, not accusations.

She moistened her dry lips.

"I was there," she said, hearing the quiver in her voice. "Constance sang. I refused to talk to the reporter. He was asked to move out of the restricted area."

She closed her eyes and continued in a monotone. "I disappeared from backstage because I went home early. I must have come in during the time you were gone."

She opened her eyes but turned from him, staring instead at the curve of black stovepipe against the brick wall. "Something also true, which isn't in the story, is that while last week I may have been a teacher, I won't be at the start of the fall semester. Not at that college. They agreed to hire me only as long as I could keep Rhee Weston completely away from their hallowed halls."

He took the newspaper from her, folded it once, and then ripped it in half.

"Damn it," he said as he pushed his chair back from the table.

She watched dispassionately as he ran his hand through his hair. A small voice inside her whispered that she ought to be screaming at the injustice of it, but it seemed pointless to scream. She had lost so much already. What was one more loss?

Anton crumpled the paper and tossed it into the trash. She watched as he paced the room. Twice he turned as though to speak, apparently thought better of it and turned away. The third time, he faced her.

Hillary didn't know what she expected him to say, but it certainly wasn't the halting invitation she heard.

"I need some air," he said. "Will you go with me? For a drive? Just for a little while."

The questions were still there in his eyes, still begging answers. But how could she answer them? She didn't even know what they were.

She felt the weight of her own exhaustion

pulling her down but knew that sleep now was impossible. She found enough strength to attempt to smile, and nodded.

Anton led her not to his pickup truck but to a heavy Lincoln, big enough to accommodate his large frame, and powerful enough to take the hills and curves without protest. With a touch of buttons he lowered the windows, letting the night air into the car with them.

He drove without speaking down the hill, through the little town of Altus, finally turning onto a gravel road. Hillary didn't need to ask where they were going. She turned in her seat, watching the clean strength of his profile as he concentrated on the road and something far removed from where they actually were.

The wind through the car cooled her, all but her burning eyes. Her hair whipped against her cheeks.

Don't do this, she wanted to tell him. *It won't do either of us any good.* But she couldn't speak, because she wanted this trip into memory, too.

She felt the air changing, growing cooler, moister as they approached the river.

He parked the car and turned to her. She opened her door and stepped outside. They met at the front of the car. She felt the surge of energy flowing between them as he held her arm to steady her in the dark walk down to the water's edge.

They were truly alone here. Far away, to the north, were the lights of the massive lock and dam, one of a series that made this inland water-way possible. Now there wasn't even traffic on the river. Here she heard not even the night noises, only the gentle lap of water against the shore.

"The little restaurant is still at the marina," Anton said softly, breaking the silence.

"Is it?" she asked. "I often wondered."

"They asked about you."

"Oh." How *had* he answered the questions? She had been so busy with her own answers, she really hadn't considered what he would say. Obviously he hadn't told them the truth, at least not all of it.

"It must have been hard for you, not saying anything."

"Hard for me?" He breathed deeply of the night air. "Yes, it was." He turned to her. A cloud passing across the moon cast shadows on his face, softening his features. "It was a lot like tonight," he said.

She felt her heart expanding, filling her chest, pushing against her ribs. But her throat was tight, so tight. It had been a night like this, silent and still. They had been alone on the boat, only the two of them in the whole world, it seemed. Alone, until they reached the marina, and alone as they returned. She was caught in that memory, as he was.

His hand tightened on her arm as he faced her in the moonlight.

Inevitable, she thought as she watched him bend toward her. Oh, Lord, it had been so long.

His lips touched hers gently, questioningly, and she gave in to her need to sway against him. With a soft sigh she captured his face in her hands.

She felt his moan as he pulled her to him and deepened the kiss.

So very, very long, she thought as she came to life beneath his touch. How could she ever put him out of her heart? It was as though no time, and yet an eternity, had passed since last he held her.

His touch resurrected all the yearnings she had ever felt for him, all the yearnings she had tried so hard to forget.

He released her mouth to kiss her eyes, her cheeks, to bury his face against her throat.

"God, I've missed you, Elaine."

She felt the warmth draining from her. Slowly she eased her hands from his neck to his chest and pushed away. She caught one glimpse of the stricken look in his eyes as she turned from him—as he let her turn.

"Hillary, I—"

"No, don't," she said. "I . . . I understand."

But did she? Could she?

She stumbled as she stepped away from him, and he caught her arm.

"Please," she whispered. "Just take me home."

Chapter Six

Hillary heard Constance's footsteps clattering down the stairs from the attic bedroom she had appropriated years before. Hurrying, she finished dressing just as Constance tapped on the door, called out and walked in.

"Good morning," Constance said cheerfully.

Hillary glanced up into the mirror at the young woman, pausing in her attempt at makeup.

"Good morning."

Constance leaned against the mantel and examined her critically. "You look like death," she said finally.

"Thanks a lot," Hillary said ruefully.

"No, I'm serious," Constance told her. She frowned as she walked to Hillary's side. "Didn't you sleep at all last night?"

Hillary sank down onto the dresser stool and sighed. "It's that obvious, is it?"

Constance nodded. She picked up the blusher and handed it to Hillary. "Try a little prepackaged health," she said. "See if that helps."

Shaking her head, Hillary took the compact from Constance. Lightly she applied color to her cheeks and turned to Constance for approval.

"More," Constance said.

"Sorry," Hillary told her, "but I'm afraid you're going to have to love me as I am this morning. I don't think anything less than a full complement of stage makeup would help, and I'm not about to wear that downstairs."

"Hillary?" Constance frowned. "I didn't mean to turn this into an awful time for you. I know there's not a lot to do here, but—"

"Don't be silly, Constance. I've had so much to do lately, I welcome the leisure."

"Yeah, but it's not agreeing with you. I didn't even think about what I could be taking you away from. I just needed you with me."

"Don't think about it," Hillary said. "You're not taking me away from anything. And if I didn't want to be with you, I wouldn't be here."

"Well—so why can't you sleep, then?" Constance asked. "You and Mom are getting along, aren't you?"

Hillary nodded. "Yes. I like Inez."

"Bill's obnoxious, but he hasn't been around all that much, so he can't be the problem."

Hillary just grinned at her.

"Well, then, it's got to be Anton. Has he said something to you? Honestly, I could break his skull sometimes."

Hillary shook her head. "Anton hasn't said anything to me, Constance." It was another lie, she thought, but a necessary one. "When has he had time to say anything to me? He's busy at the winery from before I get up until after I go to bed. Don't worry about it."

"Is it me and Tippy, then? Is that what's wrong?"

Hillary reached for the young woman's hand. "Constance, occasionally I don't sleep well. Don't start digging for a reason. Please?"

"Okay," Constance finally conceded. "If you insist." She tugged at Hillary's hand. "Come on. I'm famished."

Hillary chuckled. "I thought you were supposed to be sick."

"Maybe other people are sick," Constance said. "I starve. By the way," she added as they reached the door, "speaking of secrets, if we can grab an hour this afternoon when everybody else is busy at the winery, I'd like you to listen to something. I've got the neatest melody in my head, but I haven't been able to find time at the piano. I'd really like your help with it. And I'm no good at all with lyrics; you know that."

"Why don't you let Tippy help you with the lyrics? He's pretty good with them."

Constance stopped on the stairs, tracing her fingers over the banister. A soft smile transformed her face. "Yes, he is, isn't he?"

Hillary laughed. "When you said you were starving, I thought you meant for food."

Constance grinned. "Yeah. That, too."

They were both smiling when they pushed into

the kitchen. Hillary's smile melted from her. Anton leaned back against the cabinet, holding a coffee cup in one hand. Hillary stopped just inside the door, in a repeat of the previous night's actions. Instinctively, she took a step backward and then stopped. No, she couldn't do that.

They stared at each other from across the room. Slowly he lowered his cup to the countertop.

Constance looked from Hillary to Anton. She raised one eyebrow inquisitively, and then fixed an impudent grin on her face.

"Say good morning, brother."

Hillary watched his eyes darken.

"Good morning," he said stiffly.

"Good," Constance said, turning. "Say good morning, Hillary."

Hillary glanced sharply at Constance but saw only determination in the young woman's expression.

"Good morning," she said.

"Now," Constance said, placing her hands on her hips, "you're both supposed to smile."

Anton turned abruptly. "I'm late," he said.

"Anton Roeffler," Constance began, "don't you dare just—" the screen door slammed shut behind him "—walk out on me," Constance finished lamely.

Hillary turned to the cabinet, hiding the hurt she felt under the actions of reaching for dishes and silverware. How long could they go on this way?

"Honestly!" Constance said. "I don't know what's gotten into him. If I treated a guest of his like he's treating you, he'd switch my legs."

Hillary tried to smile. "He may yet, Constance. These aren't exactly *usual* circumstances."

"No." Constance sighed deeply as she reached for a cup. "They aren't, are they? I really didn't think he'd stay mad this long, though."

Hillary saw the glimmer of tears in the young woman's eyes.

"Connie," Hillary said softly, "your brother loves you. I don't think he's still angry with you."

"No, but he's disappointed in me, and that's just . . . just about as bad, because I'm not sorry for anything I've done. Oh, Hillary," she cried, "what a mess things are in. I really expected Anton to understand. You didn't know my dad. He was always grim and unbending, even when I was little. Harvest was almost as good as Christmas, because those were the only times Anton came home from school. And when he was here, he was more father to me than . . . than he was brother. He made toys for me."

The tears spilled from Constance's eyes. "He was the one I went to when I skinned my knee, or broke my doll, or had my feelings hurt. He always made it better."

Constance's voice broke. "I don't want to hide things from him. I want him to be happy for me!"

Hillary wanted to comfort her, to tell her that what she wanted would happen, but she wasn't at all sure that could ever be.

"Have you thought," she asked hesitantly, "that maybe something else is bothering him?"

Constance sniffed and smiled at her. "I *know* something else is bothering him. I just don't know what."

But I know, Hillary thought. Should she tell her? Would it help, or would it only make the remaining week even more unbearable?

"Finish your coffee," Constance said, breaking into her thoughts, "and I'll give you the fifty-cent tour before the tasting room opens. We could both use some fresh air."

CONSTANCE LED HER DOWN the back stairs to the cellar beneath the house. It was cool and dry, and empty now except for a few shelves with neatly labeled boxes.

"This is where it all began," Constance said. "Well, not actually *here*. The first cellar was about a half mile east of here. You can still see the ruins of the cabin that covered it, over on what is Bill's place now. But at one time the entire winery was under this house."

Hillary glanced around. It was a spacious cellar, but she couldn't imagine it housing a winery and storage.

Constance grinned at her. "It grew a little over the years, but it wasn't much larger when Anton took over. Although," she added, grinning, "it was a little bigger than two barrels in the basement. Grandpa dug a new cellar. It's part of the complex we use now. Come on."

Hillary followed her out into the brightness of the morning, but instead of going toward the winery Constance turned to the left.

"We'd only get in the way down there," she said, "and they might even put us to work."

Constance took a path through the trees surrounding the house and into the fields. In the distance, harvesters were busy. An occasional shout, a laugh, the sound of a tractor engine floated to them.

"Can you imagine what it was like a hundred years ago?" Constance asked. "Without the tractors? Without the power equipment to dig the cellars? Doing everything by hand or with a mule? I get all shivery thinking about the challenges those first immigrants faced. My great-great-grandfather could barely speak English when he came here. He hacked a farm out of the wilderness, dug his cellar by hand, planted each one of his vines himself, harvested by hand. He was in a strange country, with a strange language. By the standards of the people already here, he and the other settlers practiced a religion that was different. But he stayed. He raised eight children. He outlived three wives. And he made something out of this wild land." Constance turned in a wide circle, gesturing with both arms. "I think he'd be proud of what Anton has done here."

"It has to be—comforting—to know that your family has been in one place for a hundred years, and will probably always be there," Hillary said. "My father is military, or he was until he retired. I don't think we ever lived in one place longer than two years."

"It is comforting," Constance said, "but it's also kind of frightening. There's a responsibility on you to live up to your heritage, not to throw away what someone else has worked so hard to build, like so many of the families have. Do you know there used to be over a hundred wineries in Arkansas?"

Hillary glanced up. "No, I didn't know that."

Constance nodded. "Yes. After the repeal of Prohibition. I'm not saying how good they were, but they *were*. And now there are less than two dozen left. And a lot of the old ones, the really old ones, have been closed. And a lot of the acreage that used to be devoted to vines has been plowed up or allowed to go wild.

"But," Constance said, shrugging, "what's left is quality. Wouldn't you say so, Hillary?" she asked, grinning.

Hillary grinned back. Constance already knew how much she didn't know about grapes. "Of course."

"This was Grandpa's standard vine," Constance said. "It's called Campbell's Early. It makes a nice, inexpensive red table wine. And that over there," she said as she pointed, "is a muscat."

"They all look the same to me, Constance."

"They don't after you've planted and picked and pruned them for a few years. They each have their own personalities. Come on. I want to show you something else."

They walked north, avoiding the harvesters, until they stood in a high field.

"The Chardonnay," Constance said, pointing to her left. "Anton's really proud of that. His wine won an honorable mention at the Eastern wine-growers' judging at Lancaster the first year he entered it. It's almost unheard of to do that. And his Cynthiana consistently brings home prizes. All of us here on the hill are working very hard to upgrade our product, and while we might laugh among ourselves about exporting Arkansas wines to California and Europe, it's something we're only partially teasing about. But that's not why I brought you up here."

"No?" Hillary asked. "I was kind of enjoying the lesson."

"Did I get on my soapbox again? I have a habit of doing that, you know."

"No, I didn't know, Constance."

"It's hard for me not to," Constance said. "My father never let me forget that I was adopted."

"I didn't..."

But Constance didn't let her finish her surprised stammer.

"Well, it just doesn't come up in conversation very often. You don't just throw out, 'By the way, I was adopted,' but...but it makes a difference, knowing, and even knowing why, you know—that Mom missed Florence so much she, well, she joked about it. She said she was outnumbered with all the men in the house. Anyway, even if I am adopted, I feel like a Roeffler, and I love this land. But even loving it as much as I do, it's got to be just a little shadow of what Anton feels for it. You know, he's worked his whole life for this place? He was still in college when Dad died."

Hillary listened enthralled as she heard of a side of him she had only imagined.

"He almost quit school. I heard him and Mom talking about it. You know, he's always wanted to be a winegrower. He was so disappointed with the way Dad let the place run down. Anyway, when he did come home, he started working on the place, and he hasn't stopped yet. He bought out Ben and Timothy's interest, and when he paid for that, he dug the new cellars, and when he paid for them, he just kept putting the money back in, and he kept putting himself in. You know?"

Hillary nodded, not speaking.

"It was almost," Constance said, "as though he were driven. I want you to understand him just a little bit, Hillary."

Hillary looked up. She felt dangerously close to tears, but she hid that from Constance. "I think I do," she said.

"No, you can't. Because the Anton you've seen this week isn't . . . well, he just isn't acting like my brother, and I wanted you to know that. I wanted you to know a little bit more about him. I don't want you to hate him."

Hillary reached for Constance's hand. "I don't hate him, Constance."

"No. But you don't *like* him.

Like him? No, she didn't like him, not this Anton. But the one she had met before, the one that Constance was trying so hard to explain to her— yes. First she had liked him.

"Constance, don't worry about it, please."

"But I do! Do you know, once I thought the only thing he really loved was this land. That was when he was first starting to build. When he was buying out our brothers' interest. The court made him my guardian, and I was ready to fight. I didn't want to sell my part. He didn't even ask. He told me, *told me*, that he wanted me to wait until I was twenty-one to decide what I wanted to do with my share. And each year my part gets to be worth more, and more, and it's all because of his hard work.

"Hillary, there's a part of him that he keeps hidden away, like there's a part of you that you keep hidden, that he only lets people very close to him see. And that part is wonderful, Hillary, warm and loving and understanding, and that's the part of him I want you to know."

Hillary turned, pretending to look back at the house. Oh, yes, she had seen that part of him. Her throat tightened, and tears threatened to spill from her eyes. But she doubted she would ever see it again.

ANTON STEPPED BACK from the loading dock as another trailer, now empty, pulled away. He watched the activity around him as his workers competently started this load of grapes on its involved route to becoming wine.

It was a good harvest, better even than he had expected. And, better, too, for all of his neighbors. Except for Bill, he thought. But he didn't want to think about Bill now, or the Roeffler land going to waste.

Without the new equipment he had added this year, without the extra casks waiting now in the cellars, he would never have been able to handle his grapes and those he had promised to buy. But he could handle them, he thought with satisfaction. And while a capacity of a half-million gallons didn't make Roeffler's a giant in the wine industry, it was a start.

He saw his mother approaching and walked to her side.

She studied his face, frowning slightly, with a solicitude he supposed she would never lose. She smiled at him.

"Debbie just called from the tasting room. They've had a tour bus pull up front, and she needs some help."

Anton glanced once again at the activity around him. "I don't have anyone I can spare right now. Where is Constance?"

"It was so slow earlier, Debbie told her she could handle it by herself. She's probably out in the yard, because she didn't answer the telephone."

"Great," he said. "Well, give me a minute here, to make sure things are running smoothly, and I'll go up and look for her."

"Anton," his mother said as he turned.

"Yes?"

"Take time to eat some lunch while you're gone. I can watch things for a while."

HE HEARD THE PIANO as he approached the house. Someone was playing a light, lilting melody. He let himself in quietly and stood in the living-room doorway, watching them, unobserved.

Constance sat on the bench at the Steinway, playing. Hillary stood behind her, slightly to her left. He let himself look at her, really look at her, for the first time since she arrived.

She looked slim and innocent, and even more desirable than he had remembered, in the soft green terry-cloth shorts and matching top, with her hair pulled back and caught with a clasp at the back of her neck.

Who was she, he wondered. Surely she wasn't the scheming seductress he'd tried to label her. She should never have come back. His wounds were still too raw for him to meet her like a stranger. After all this time, just the sight of her had thrown him back into wanting her, hating her and loving what he had thought she was.

"That's beautiful," he heard Hillary say. "I think you ought to keep about eight bars just as it is before you pick up the tempo and bring in the bass. Tippy is going to love it."

Anton jerked upright. What was she doing? Encouraging Constance? Leading her even farther into the web she had woven?

"Constance!" Her name grated harshly in the

room. Too harshly, he realized, but he couldn't recall it.

Both women turned. Hillary had the grace, at least, to look startled and embarrassed, Constance only defiant.

"Debbie has a tour bus. She needs your help."

Constance scooted off the piano bench and started out of the room.

"Wait," Hillary told her. "I'll go with you."

"No," Anton said. "You and I need to talk."

Constance stopped in her march to the door. "Look, Anton," she said. "If you're upset with me, say it to me. Don't take it out on Hillary. I asked her to help me."

"And she was only too happy to help, wasn't she?"

"Yes!" Constance said. "She's always been happy to help me. What is so wrong with that?"

Maybe he should have told her long ago. Secrets. Deceptions. Lies. He was sick of them all. But it wasn't only his secret.

"I'm not angry with you," he said. "But there is a busload of people waiting."

"Go on, Constance," Hillary urged. "It's all right."

Constance glanced dubiously at the two of them.

"A busload," Anton reminded her.

"Oh, all right," she said and flounced from the room.

Hillary waited hesitantly by the piano. He listened until he heard the door slam.

She might have helped keep Constance here, but what good was it doing if she constantly kept alive an impossible fantasy? Damn her! How could she look so innocent and be so devious? Anger helped. Anger masked the pain of betrayal he felt each time he looked at her.

"And are you happy to help?" he asked. "Eager and willing to ruin a young girl's life?"

He saw her straighten and steel herself.

"I am happy to help," she said brittlely. "Help Constance be the woman she can be."

"This isn't working," he said. "Without your interference, she would realize that that life is wrong for her."

"My interference?" Hillary cried.

"Your interference," he interrupted. "You're encouraging her to believe that this man really does love her, that he's going to marry her, that life with him is going to be wonderful."

"Tippy does love her! Is that what this is all about? Did you think that you'd get her here for two weeks and she'd forget about a life she's chosen for herself? It won't work, Anton. She's serious about this. And Tippy does love her."

"Tippy," he said, hating the images it called up. "What kind of name is that for a man?"

Hillary glared at him from across the room. "It's the best a six-year-old could do in a south-side Oklahoma City grade school with a name like Tipton Peterson Grey III. That's what kind of name it is. Just as yours would be Tony if you had gone to public school in Altus, Arkansas, instead of being shipped to the Benedictine monks across the river with the rest of you—bigots!''

Her anger reached him. Where nothing else had, her anger touched him. Bigot? Was that what she really thought of him? But even as he wondered, he watched her crumple onto the bench.

She buried her face in her hands. "I'm sorry," she said. "You didn't deserve that. But you've got to understand. Constance is *not* going to change. She's chosen a life that's right for her. One she wants. One that she can excel in. Don't you know how much she loves you? Don't you know how much she wants you to approve of her?''

She looked up at him. "Don't drive her away, Anton. Don't force her to choose between you and Tippy.''

As Hillary had. A newscast, printed indelibly on his memory, flashed to life before his eyes. Hillary and Tippy leaving the courthouse in Nashville, being mobbed by the press. Tippy Grey's arm tightening around Hillary while he pushed a reporter out of the way. Anton should have been there protecting her, not some pompous, strutting fool. He couldn't stop the words.

"Constance isn't you, Hillary. Don't be so sure of her choice.''

He watched Hillary's eyes widen and saw her body tense, almost as though he had actually struck her. He hadn't meant to let his bitterness show. Instantly he wanted to call back the words, even as he wanted to take her in his arms and tell her he was sorry.

Take her in his arms? God, how he wanted to do that.

Therein lies the way to madness, he thought.

There were shadows in her eyes, shadows he had once been fool enough to think he could erase. He felt no satisfaction in knowing that now he had helped put them there.

He turned and left the room.

Chapter Seven

Hillary remained on the piano bench. She had once read that shock victims don't feel their own pain. That must be what it is, she thought. Shock. Because she knew she had just been dealt a lethal blow. Some part of her had just been severed—neatly, cleanly, without a drop of blood being spilled. But when feeling returned, she knew it wouldn't be painless. If feeling returned.

She turned numbly toward the keyboard. Music. Music would help. It always helped. She closed her eyes as she placed her fingers on the keys. Bach, yes, definitely Bach.

The first thunderous chords sounded around her. She drew in a deep breath. She needed an organ for this, the organ at the church, where the music could vibrate the walls. But the Steinway would do.

She gave herself up to the fugue, pouring her soul into it.

Anton stopped when he heard the first notes thunder from the house and roll through the air.

He turned and listened. Bach? Never before had he heard music like this coming from that piano. And never before had he suspected Hillary, fragile as she seemed, capable of reproducing this pounding, turbulent music, echoing the torment in his own soul.

Drawn, he followed the sound toward its source. Through the open curtains he saw her, lost in the music. Saw the first tears as they squeezed from beneath her tightly closed eyes. Saw her hands crash on the keys in violent discord. Saw her turn, stumble from the bench, and run from the room.

Hillary ran for the privacy of her bedroom. She slammed the door behind her and collapsed on the bed, clutching the pillow to her.

Painless? No. Oh, no. It wasn't painless. How could anything that had happened so long ago, that had ended so long ago, still have the power to hurt so much? But it hadn't ended for her. She knew that, had known it all along. The only thing that had ever died was Anton's love for her. Died? No. She had killed it. Killed it, and his ability to trust her.

She had promised herself that nothing that had happened could ever make her cry again, but she was wrong, so wrong.

She had known it was over, known there could be no chance for them. But why, God, why, had it needed to be demonstrated so vividly? How could she ever forget the suspicion and distrust in Anton's eyes, in his voice, in his cutting words.

Look at me! she had wanted to scream. I'm real,

I am a decent person, not the ogre you think I am. *Believe me!*

But it wouldn't do any good. Nothing she ever said or did would change what she had made him think of her.

"Hillary."

Anton's hoarse voice held her prisoner. She felt the subtle shifting of the bed as he sat beside her and the lightest of touches as he brushed his fingers along her shoulder.

"Hillary?"

Was that pain she heard in his voice? Good! she thought. He deserved it. No. No, he didn't. But neither did she.

"Please," she whispered, not looking at him, "please, just leave me alone."

"I can't do that," he said.

Then she felt his hands, gentle in their strength, lifting her, turning her, until she was pressed against his chest.

"Don't cry. Not anymore."

She ought to push away. She knew that. But she had wanted him to hold her this way for so long.

One trembling hand tangled in her hair, holding her cheek still against his heart. The other moved hesitantly, tentatively over her back, her shoulders.

Caught in the safety of his arms, Hillary couldn't stop her tears, couldn't stop her sobs. She slid her arms around him, needing his strength, as the pain of having lost him washed through her.

"Hillary." She heard the emotion that thickened his voice. "I never meant to say those words. I'd never hurt you. Not deliberately."

"I know," she said. She caught her lower lip between her teeth and tried to steady her breathing. There were so many things she wanted to tell him, needed him to believe. "And I never meant to hurt you. I did love you." Her flood of words could no longer be dammed. "I didn't lie about that. When I left you, I left part of me here. I didn't want to leave you. I never wanted to leave."

A fresh paroxysm of grief caught her and she gave in to it, too weak not to.

He caught her face in his hands and lifted it to his.

"Ssh," he murmured. "Please. Don't do this."

She felt the soft brush of his mustache as his lips moved over her forehead and touched her eyes.

"I loved you so much," she whispered, "wanted you so much. I used to lie awake at night, aching for you. You never understood why I pulled away. Anton, I know how you feel about marriage. I couldn't add that to all the other wrongs. I knew I was going to lose you."

Her voice caught, and broke. "It all seemed so innocent. The first lie was—"

"Ssh," he murmured again before his mouth captured hers and silenced her.

Warmth spiraled through her body. She met his kiss hungrily, greedily, the love within her demanding expression. And if he would not let her voice it, could he deny what she told him with her actions?

She felt the change in his heartbeat, felt his muscles tensing beneath her hands. Then the weight of him was bearing her down, and he followed her, the desperation in his touch matching that in hers.

She moaned as she felt his hand find her breast. "Oh, yes," she murmured.

Could it be so wrong to love him? To give him the love she had denied him, denied herself, so long before? No. No, it couldn't, she thought.

She caught his hand with hers, holding it to her as she pressed herself closer to him, as she answered the aggressive search of his lips, his tongue, with her own.

They lay tangled on the bed, each inch of her pressed by his weight, his lean strength holding her still. She worked her fingers beneath his shirt. She needed the touch of his flesh.

She moaned when he tore his mouth from hers. Breathing heavily, he buried his face against her throat. He was steadying himself, she knew. Withdrawing from her. He was a master at that, she remembered, able to mask his emotions, his heart, with chilling control. But she wasn't, not anymore.

"Love me," she whispered. "Oh, please love me."

He groaned against her throat. It seemed an eternity before his lips began their slow search downward. He eased the strap from her shoulder, lowering the terry-cloth bodice until her breast was exposed to his seeking mouth.

"Oh, yes." Her words were little more than a whimper.

She moved beneath him, wanting to touch him, needing to touch him, until, as though freed from some restraint, he sighed against her. His mouth returned to hers, while his hands began an exquisite torture of her body.

She felt his callused hand rasp along the softness of her thigh and then the coolness of the air against her heated skin as he lifted her top and eased it from her. Her fingers fumbled with the buttons of his shirt.

"No," he murmured. "Not yet. We've waited so long for this. Don't rush. Don't rush."

His mouth returned to her breast, drawing her into a vortex of pleasure so intense she thought she must scream from it. His hands slid inside the waistband of her shorts, cupping her hips, pulling her to him.

Don't rush? she thought, as she moaned against his throat. She forced herself not to pull at him, not to demand more than he was willing to give, to let him set the pace, until every cell in her body was tingling from his attention and crying out for fulfillment, until at last they had shed the last barrier of clothing between them and each touch of her flesh was met by the answering touch of his, until at last he joined their bodies and she cried out in longing and in desperation.

"I love you, Anton. I do love you."

Then, because words were no longer possible, she again let her body say what she could not— moving with him, taking pleasure, giving pleasure until she was capable of nothing but feeling—a pleasure so intense it bordered on pain, tightening her body, lifting her against him, blinding her with its brightness, deafening her with its roar. A moan caught in her throat and then echoed in the room as she collapsed, quivering beneath him.

She heard his answering groan and caught his mouth with hers, taking his breath into her.

He held her until the last tremor racked her body; then, easing his weight from her, he rolled to one side, taking her with him, holding her.

No. The thought darted incoherently through her. This couldn't be wrong. This magic between them could never be wrong.

He was beautiful, she thought between shuddering breaths, more beautiful than she had imagined. She lifted her hand and let her fingers drop to the long lean muscles of his thigh.

And giving. He was even more giving than she had imagined.

She turned in his arms only enough to be able to place a swift kiss on the moist, heated flesh over his still-racing heart.

Now, without the weight of him covering her, the air conditioning that cooled the house during the daytime chilled her damp body. She shivered.

Anton reached across her, pulled the bedspread up over the edge of the bed, and covered her with it.

"Did I hurt you?" he asked. "I tried to be...I meant to be gentle."

Hillary gave a contented little chuckle against his chest. Gentle? Yes. And as intense as a summer storm. She twisted to look at his face. "I won't break, Anton," she said softly. "I promise."

He traced his fingers along her cheek. "No," he said, "but you do bruise."

She watched his eyes cloud.

"Those bruises?" he asked in the same soft, low voice. "You didn't get those when you ran the car off the road, did you?"

She closed her eyes against the questions in his, against the memories his words recalled.

"No."

His arm tightened possessively around her while she listened to the steady thud of his heartbeat.

"Tell me about...Elaine," he said finally.

Elaine? Hillary wondered. The woman Anton had thought she was, or the woman whose name she had borrowed? Or both?

Both, Hillary decided, searching for words to voice what she didn't completely understand. "Elaine Grey was my stepmother," she said. "Tippy's mother." She felt Anton tense at the name and looked up at him, her eyes pleading for his patience with her halting explanation. "I don't know why she married my father unless it was because she thought Tippy needed a steadying influence in his life. He was in junior high school then, thirteen and heading for trouble. And my father was attractive. He still is. He just has no heart. I don't know if he buried it with my mother, or if he never had one." Hillary sighed deeply. "Maybe she loved him. She stayed with him for three years. I was away in college most of the time, but those vacations, those holidays, were the only times I felt that I really had a home. She's a beautiful woman," Hillary told him, "gracious and charming. And she was the first person who ever made me feel as though I were truly loved. She was the first person who ever made me feel that my love was valued. She was the first person who ever made me feel as if I were part of a family. When she gave up on my father, she made sure I knew she wasn't giving up on me. That's why, when I needed a name that wouldn't be recognized, couldn't be traced, I knew she wouldn't mind if I borrowed hers. And that's why, when I needed a place to hide, after I returned, I went to her."

"You wouldn't take my phone calls," Anton said, not accusing, she recognized, but groping.

"No."

"But you saw Bill."

She felt her defenses tightening and willed them to relax. "The desk didn't tell me his full name. Just Mr. Roeffler. I thought..." She remembered for one moment her fleeting sense of relief and the sharp twist of disappointment. "I thought he was you. That's the only way he got upstairs."

"He said you were in Tippy Grey's apartment. In your robe. Obviously just out of bed."

Hillary sighed deeply. She'd wondered what kind of story Bill had brought back. All she could do was try to explain.

"Tippy has an army of security people," she said softly. "No one could get through without approval, no one. Especially not reporters. We had just found out about Jay's death. The doctor had given me a tranquilizer. I tried to sleep. Elaine was in the next room. I asked her to give me a few minutes alone with an old friend."

"He said..." Anton hesitated. "He said you tried to seduce him."

Hillary moaned against Anton's chest. So that was what he had said. "Your cousin," she told him quietly, "is not a very nice man. Nor is he a truthful one. I had him thrown out of the apartment."

She remembered bitterly how Bill had tried to force her to buy his silence.

"You didn't believe him?" she whispered.

"I didn't know what to believe then, Hillary." Anton drew a deep breath, and then, as though realizing the strength in his arms, eased his grip on her. "I think at that point I wanted to believe him. It was easier to hate you; I wanted to hate you. I think for a while I must have been just a little bit crazy, because there was a time when I wanted you to hurt. I wanted to know that you felt just a fraction of the pain that I did."

He tilted her face to his. She wanted to ease the troubled lines from around his eyes, but she lay still.

"But that didn't last long, Hillary. And I'm ashamed for ever feeling it."

"Don't be," she whispered, touching her fingers to his mouth. "Oh, don't be. Not ever. Not because of something I put in motion."

He kissed the tips of her fingers and then bent to her, capturing her in a kiss that was both violent and purging.

"You don't have to lie to me, ever again," he said. "And you don't ever have to tell me something just because you think it's what I want to hear."

Was that what he thought she had done?

"Never, Anton," she whispered, and then she remembered the one untruth already between them, the one she couldn't speak of, the one Constance would have to tell him.

"Anton..."

"Ssh," he murmured. "Now is all we have. Let's not waste it with words."

"Anton," she moaned before his mouth closed on hers and he silenced her, taking her with him on a journey filled with desperation and broken dreams.

ANTON TRIED. Hillary did have to give him credit for that. That evening when the workers left, instead of remaining at the winery, he returned to the house.

As he walked into the kitchen, Inez looked up from the salad she and Constance were preparing.

"Well, well," she said to her son. "Is it exhaustion or just good sense that brings you home this early?"

"A little bit of both," Anton told her, grinning. "And hunger. Do I have time to clean up before supper?"

Inez glanced at Hillary and then back at Anton. "Fifteen minutes," she said, smiling. "Not a second longer."

"Right," he said. Only Hillary noticed his questioning glance at her as he left the room.

Inez dropped her hands into her lap and sat staring at the doorway he had just walked through, a bemused smile on her face. She shook her head and pushed back from the table.

"I think we'll use the dining room tonight," she said as she reached for a key on the rack near the door. "Would you mind going down to the tasting room for me, Hillary? A little wine might be nice, too."

"Of course I'll go," Hillary said. "What kind do you want me to bring back?"

Inez glanced around the kitchen. "The Cynthiana, I think," she said. "I just can't abide that dry stuff, even if he is so proud of it. I like something with a little bit more flavor."

Hillary chuckled as she caught the teasing glint in Inez's eyes. The woman had been born into a winemaking family and had raised a winemaking family. She had earned the right to be outspoken in her tastes if she wanted to be.

"The Cynthiana it is," Hillary said, laughing.

When she returned with the wine, she found the cherry dining-room table set with fine old china and cut crystal stemware waiting. She went on through to the kitchen and handed the wine to Inez.

"Do I have time to change?" Hillary asked.

Inez shook her head. "We won't dress for dinner. Not tonight."

She took a cork puller from the drawer and deftly opened one of the bottles. Pouring a small amount of wine into a glass, she sipped it in a studied parody of the tasting ritual.

"Excellent bouquet," Inez said. She returned the bottle to Hillary. "Would you put this in the dining room, please?"

As Hillary started for the door, Anton entered. He wore soft, faded jeans, a pair of Mexican huaraches and a baseball shirt bearing the name "Post" in a familiar red circle, a bunch of grapes and the words, "It's not just for breakfast anymore!"

Inez choked back a laugh, and Constance, walking into the kitchen behind her brother, giggled.

"Advertising for the competition, Anton?" his mother asked.

Anton's smile encompassed his mother and his sister. "I couldn't resist. When I got out of the shower, I found this laid out, waiting for me. I don't suppose any of you know who put it on my bed, do you?"

Constance sidled around her brother, eyeing him critically. "Jealousy," she said. "I think that's why you're wearing it. I bet you wish you'd thought of it first."

Anton grinned at her. "Listen, twerp. Somehow, 'Roefflers—It's not just for breakfast anymore,' doesn't quite have the same ring."

Hillary relaxed against the cabinet. No sign of Anton's disappointment in Constance was evident, and Constance was glowing under his gentle teasing. Hillary breathed a small prayer of thanks.

The mood lasted through dinner and afterward. When the last dish was dried and put away, the four of them gathered in the living room.

"That was a beautiful melody you were playing this afternoon, Constance," Anton said.

Constance looked up, alarm in her eyes, but Anton continued in the same easy manner.

"I don't believe I've heard it before."

"No," Constance said guardedly. "That was the first time I've been able to get it out of my head and onto the piano."

"You wrote it?" he asked in surprise. He glanced at Hillary, who nodded, almost imperceptibly. *Please,* she thought, *don't let him say anything to hurt Constance.*

"Yes," Constance told him. A note of defiance crept into her voice. "I've written quite a few."

Hillary saw Anton's eyes begin to darken.

"Would you play it for me, Constance?" Inez interrupted.

Hillary glanced at her gratefully.

"I'd love to hear it," the woman said.

Constance glanced at her mother and at her brother warily. "Sure," she said at last. "I'd like you to hear it."

She played the melody, as pure and clean as a spring morning, and then turned to face her family.

"It is beautiful," Inez said. "I had no idea you have that kind of talent. I'm proud of you."

Anton frowned slightly. "But as pretty as it is, Constance, why would you want to..." He repeated Hillary's words of that afternoon, "Why would you want to pick up the tempo and bring in the bass?"

A hesitant smile worried Constance's lips. "Because it may be beautiful, Anton, but it isn't commercial the way it is."

"And does it have to be commercial?" he asked, still frowning.

"It does," Constance told him, picking out with one finger the basic melody, "if I want more than my family and a few friends to hear it."

"I see," Anton said finally.

But Hillary wondered, did he really?

HE CAME TO HER THAT NIGHT and all thought of refusing him fled when she saw the hunger in his eyes and felt the need in his touch.

But still later, as she lay sleepless in his arms while the breeze from the open window kissed them and as the night noises serenaded them, she wondered how much of what she had tried to tell

Irresistible!

YOURS FREE FOR KEEPS!

Use the edge of a coin to rub off the box at right and reveal your surprise gift →

DEAR READER:

We would like to send you 4 Harlequin American Romances just like the one you're reading plus a surprise gift – all **ABSOLUTELY FREE**.

If you like them, we'll send you 4 more books each month to preview. Always before they're available in stores. Always for less than the regular retail price. Always with the right to cancel and owe nothing.

In addition, you'll receive **FREE** . . .
- our monthly newsletter HEART TO HEART
- our magazine ROMANCE DIGEST
- fabulous bonus books and surprise gifts
- special-edition Harlequin Bestsellers to preview for ten days without obligation

So return the attached Card and start your Harlequin honeymoon today.

Sincerely

Pamela Powers

Pamela Powers
for Harlequin

P.S. Remember, your 4 free novels and your surprise gift are yours to keep whether you buy any books or not.

PRINTED IN U.S.A.

4 EXCITING ROMANCE NOVELS PLUS A SURPRISE GIFT

FREE BOOKS/ SURPRISE GIFT

YES, please send me my four **FREE** Harlequin American Romances™ and my **FREE** surprise gift. Then send me four brand-new Harlequin American Romances each month as soon as they come off the presses. Bill me at the low price of $2.25 each (for a total of $9.00—a saving of $1.00 off the retail price). There are no shipping, handling or other hidden costs. There is no minimum number of books I must purchase. I can always return a shipment and cancel at any time. Even if I never buy a book from Harlequin, the four free novels and the surprise gift are mine to keep forever.

154 CIA NA3T

NAME_____

ADDRESS_____APT. NO._____

CITY_____

STATE_____ZIP_____

Offer limited to one per household and not valid for present subscribers. Prices subject to change.

Mail to:
Harlequin Reader Service
2504 W. Southern Avenue,
Tempe, Arizona 85282

LIMITED TIME ONLY
Mail today and get a
SECOND MYSTERY GIFT

MAIL THIS CARD TODAY

You'll receive 4 Harlequin novels
plus a fabulous surprise gift
ABSOLUTELY FREE

Anton earlier he had really understood, really believed.

It didn't matter, she told herself as he shifted in his sleep, drawing her closer. At least it was a beginning.

Chapter Eight

And Hillary tried—tried to believe that it was, that it could be, a beginning for them in spite of all that had happened. She tried, even while knowing that at any moment a word of hers or an action of hers could bring the suspicion back into Anton's eyes, could lead him to voice the distrust she felt certain he still held for her.

Hillary awoke Sunday morning to the sound of the bells from St. Mary's Church pealing across the hilltop. She could tell by the slant of sunlight and the warm air coming through the open window that it was late. But she was rested. For the first morning in over a week she awoke feeling refreshed.

She turned in the bed and looked at the other side of it, empty now. Vaguely she remembered struggling up from a deep sleep as Anton bent over her in the half-light of early morning, telling her he had to leave.

She ran her fingers over his pillow. Was it so wrong? The question kept creeping into her thoughts. He wanted her as desperately as she wanted him. That much at least was evident. But he didn't want to hear of love. He spoke only of *now*. Could there be more? Could she take this tenuous bond between them and rebuild what they had once had?

Only if he trusted her, she thought. He would trust her, she vowed.

And if he doesn't? a small voice asked.

She caught the pillow to her and hugged it tight.

"He will," she whispered. "He has to."

HILLARY FOUND CONSTANCE in the kitchen, backed up against the wall with one sandal-shod foot propped against it. She twisted the phone cord in her hands while she held the receiver caught between her cheek and shoulder.

Hillary didn't have to ask who was on the other end of the line. Constance only got that dreamy "not really here" expression for one person.

"Say hello to Tippy for me," she said as she reached for the coffeepot. Constance grinned at her.

Hillary took her coffee to the table and tried to concentrate on the rhythmic clank of a zipper or a snap hitting the revolving dryer drum in the small adjacent utility room instead of hearing the breathless whispers and occasional soft laugh from the opposite side of the room.

It was a losing battle. Even though the words weren't clear, the tone of the conversation was. Constance was supremely confident of Tippy's love. Hillary felt a small jolt of jealousy, not because Tippy loved Constance but because she could be so sure of it.

The dryer buzzer sounded along with one final clunk of the persistent zipper, and Hillary pushed her chair back and headed gratefully toward the utility room. Folding jeans, at least right now, seemed highly preferable to eavesdropping.

Even Anton's jeans? She had to reevaluate her rash decision when she opened the dryer and saw what waited. Yes, she thought, even Anton's jeans, as she wondered at the sense of intimacy this small act evoked.

Constance took the jeans from her.

"You don't have to do that."

Hillary looked up, startled. "Oh, I didn't hear you." She reached for another pair. "It's all right. I don't mind."

"And I don't mind, either," Constance said, laughing. "I welcome all the help I can get. I just wish Mom would listen to Anton and hire someone. But Tippy wants to talk to you."

Hillary hid her grimace as she dropped the jeans back into the dryer. This morning of all mornings she didn't want to answer Tippy's questions. But she had forgotten; he was as involved in his own problems as she was. After little more than a perfunctory "How are you?" he launched into his main thought.

"Connie tells me things are better now," he said.

Better? Did Constance think one reasonably pleasant evening really made things better?

"Maybe a little," Hillary said.

"Good. Listen, I have a couple of free days in the middle of the week. I could fly in Wednesday and meet her family. That way Connie could be with me for the last show."

Oh, boy. Hillary bit back her first hurried words, remembering how impetuous Tippy could be.

"Tippy..." How could she explain? "Tippy, I don't think that would be wise."

"But Connie said..."

"Constance wants to be with you, too. I know that. But her family is still...one night of...I don't think they've really changed about anything even though they are trying to understand. You're going to need to spend more than a few hours with them, Tippy." She sighed. "A lot more."

"I want to see her, Hillary. It's been a week."

"I know. And if you really want to come, come Wednesday. But, please, for everyone's sake, don't mention taking Constance away then."

"When, Hillary? It's going to have to be soon."

Soon. Soon. Soon. The word pounded with her pulse long after she had hung up the telephone. Anton and Inez both believed Constance would change her mind. Constance and Tippy both acted as if some magic transformation would take place in another week. But no one was doing anything, just waiting to be proven right. And she didn't know what to do about it.

She heard the dryer door bang shut and hurried to help Constance with the double armload of folded clothes.

"Constance," she said, deciding she couldn't keep silent any longer, "I think you're underestimating your family's prejudice. It's not going to . . . just disappear."

Constance stood facing her. "What are you trying to say?"

The young woman's gray eyes were so clear, so trusting. Hillary thought of the suspicion that would cloud them—about her, about Tippy—if she continued.

"Only . . ." She paused. Constance had enough to worry about now without adding that burden. "Only that I think you should begin trying to explain to Anton, and to Inez, how much this means to you. Calmly. Not defensively. Not angrily. Just . . . calmly."

ANTON WATCHED THE LIGHT on his office telephone. The house line was in use, had been for over half an hour. With his mother at church, that left only Constance and Hillary in the house, and only one person, logically, on the other end of that line.

He swore and dragged his hand through his hair. Why had he even come into the office? If he hadn't, he wouldn't have seen the light, wouldn't have wondered what was being said. He wouldn't pick up the phone, because as much as he didn't want to overhear Constance talking with

Tippy, he knew that hearing Hillary's soft, throaty voice, laughing, plotting, whispering with Tippy Grey, would drive him over the edge.

He slammed out of his office, but the light still mocked him. It would, he knew, as long as he was near a telephone, able to pick it up, able to hear.

He spotted Frank Huddleston. Frank was competent—more than competent, Anton knew.

"Take over!" he called to him and headed for his truck.

The break in the fence was overgrown but still visible to someone who knew where to look. Anton didn't know what drew him here—it had been years since he had last visited the cabin—but now it was the only place he knew where he could be really alone. And he needed to be alone, at least for a few minutes.

He settled himself on the sagging stoop of the cabin, leaning against the one porch rail that would still hold his weight.

Alone. He found irony in his need for solitude. All his life he had been alone, except for that brief time with Elaine— *Damn it!* Rhee. Hillary. Whoever the hell she was!

Going back to her yesterday had been a mistake. Going back last night an even greater one. But could he stay away from her? After last night, was there any way short of hell that he could keep himself from returning to her?

The climbing roses had taken over the low yard fence, and blackberry canes made a solid wall in front of the chimney, just as Florence had told

him they would all those years before when she
had brought him here and spun her romantic,
teenaged stories about the Roeffler men and their
women, and about her life as it would be.

"Well, Florence," he said softly, "it seems I
didn't break the pattern, either."

He thought of the first Roeffler, the man who
had built this cabin for himself and a bride much
too tender for this untamed land, a bride who
didn't live to raise her children or to enjoy the
comfort of the house that was planned for her. He
thought of his grandfather, loving the woman
who became Bill's grandmother. He thought of
his own father, using his mother's love for him to
drain the life from her until she was old before her
time, and of his turning away from Florence when
she needed him until she died before her time.

There were tears in this place, just as Florence
had told him when he was young, too young to
understand what she meant, but—he eased back
against the post—there was laughter here, too. It
whispered in the air around him, lingered in the
doorway from which the door had long since fallen.

"Hillary." Her name whispered from him,
trembling among the laughter and the tears.

She gave so much...or did she? For a while,
lost in her, he had forgotten all the lies. For a
while, lost in her, he had forgotten the loneliness.

Her explanations seemed so logical, so innocent, when he held her. Were they? He could only
wait and see, and protect himself as best he could.

He laughed harshly. He suspected it was too late for that. But he would protect Constance, it she would only let him.

He let his glance wander to the overgrown fields. Maybe this would be the year to approach Bill about buying his land. He could afford it now, and Bill was looking covetously at a new Corvette. God knew he would need something, anything, to fill his life when Hillary left him—again.

DINNER THAT EVENING was casual, served at the round table in the kitchen, and Anton again found time to join them.

Hillary watched the interaction between brother and sister, recognizing their tentative attempts at communication, but mindful of Anton's comment about her interference, she only entered the conversation when directly asked a question, and then very carefully. Inez, though pleasant, was silent for most of the meal.

Again they gathered in the living room, which was apparently a nightly occurrence when not interrupted by the pressures of harvest.

Constance seated herself at the piano and played softly—selections from Brahms, from Chopin— and Hillary could tell from the contented expression on Inez's face that those selections had been made with her in mind.

From all outward appearances, it was a quiet, peaceful family gathering, but Hillary noticed the signs of frustration Constance was trying so hard to hide as well as the questions in Anton's eyes when she glanced up to find him watching her.

Smoothly Constance's hands moved over the keyboard, shifting into a melody unfamiliar to Hillary—sweet, but without much character.

Hillary glanced at the young woman in time to see her chin jut out just a fraction.

"I wrote this one four years ago," Constance said, "when I was still in high school. It isn't very good."

Inez glanced sharply at her son before schooling her features into a smile and turning to her daughter. "But Constance, it's beautiful."

Constance shook her head. "No, Mom. Thank you, but it isn't. It sounds like something a high-school girl would write, all syrupy sweet with no real form and no real direction." She looked at her brother, and a defiant grin crossed her face. "Those aren't my words, Anton. I believe I heard you say them about a wine you tried once."

Hillary watched his frown of concentration change to surprise and then to a smile of soft amusement. "I think you're being a little harsh on yourself," he said, "but I understand the comparison."

"Good," Constance said as the beginning of a smile touched her lips.

With a smooth transition, she began another melody. "This one is better," she said softly. "At least with this one I knew where I wanted to go. I just didn't have the skill to get there."

It was a beautiful performance, Hillary thought as she watched, hoping that Anton and Inez realized the growth Constance exhibited as she showed them a chronological progression of her work. Most of the music now was familiar to Hillary, although Constance remained with the simple arrangements.

Constance's fingers fell still on the keys. She faced her brother earnestly. "Music is my life, Anton. It's food and drink and breath and dreams to me. It comes in all sizes and shades. It can be as insipid as the first piece I played for you. It can be light and delicate, almost seeming to have no substance until you examine the underlying structure. Or—" she poised her fingers over the keys "—like your burgundy, it can be rich and full-bodied."

Hillary sat up in shock as she heard the first chords. She cast a furtive glance at Anton, who seemed as stunned as she. *Constance wrote this?* Full-bodied it certainly was. Hillary could imagine it orchestrated—a lush, rich arrangement.

Constance played only one verse, one chorus, then sat very still. Almost visibly she gathered strength and faced her family.

"Tippy has promised me that song will be on his next album," she said distinctly and then held up her hands in front of her as though to ward off any comment. "He's written the lyrics for it. It's a beautiful song. And neither one of us has anything to be ashamed of because it's commercial, because it's popular—because *it is good.* I knew what emotion I wanted to convey. I was able to do it."

Hillary watched Anton start to speak and then force himself to be silent.

Constance turned back to the piano, picking out the melody of the song she had played the night before. Hillary watched the young woman swallow once and stare out the window.

Well, she had told her to begin talking to her family. This wasn't quite what she had envisioned, but the simple dignity in Constance's actions and words showed much more maturity than Hillary had given her credit for.

Constance swallowed again. "I met Tippy a year ago last Christmas."

Oh, Lord, Hillary thought. How much of this could the other two tolerate at one time?

But Constance had apparently steeled herself for this moment.

"We had been rehearsing for the Christmas program," she continued. "I was having trouble with one of the selections, so I asked Hillary to help me with it. After rehearsal we went to her home. And Tippy was there. I was tongue-tied and awestruck and all those gauche things I thought I was much too old for. I didn't even know he was her brother until then."

Constance laughed at the memory. "But it was awfully hard to stay awestruck when she treated him just as you treat me, Anton. And he treated me just as you treat me. By the time he walked me back to the dorm I could almost look at him as a . . . as a real person. And the next time I saw him it was easier. And the next time, easier still.

"We talked a lot about music, because that's the only thing we knew we had in common at first. He proposed just before Christmas of this year."

Constance's hands were still now, but she continued staring out the window. "I knew you wouldn't approve until you got to know him, so I asked him to wait. He's waited eight months. I want you to like him. I want both of you to like him. But we will be married."

Constance swiveled on the bench to face her brother. "Because I love him," she said softly. "And he loves me."

"Constance..." Inez began.

Constance rose from the bench and stood very straight, very tall. "No, Mom," she said, smiling hesitantly. "Not tonight. Please."

She held on to her composure until she reached the hallway and then Hillary heard her steps flying up the stairs.

Inez looked first at Anton, then, searchingly, at Hillary. "Excuse me," she said, getting to her feet, "I..." Hillary caught the glimmer of a tear in the older woman's eyes. "I..."

There was more than a little simple dignity in the house tonight, Hillary thought as she watched Inez walk from the room.

"Well," Anton said, releasing his breath and leaning back in the chair. He shook his head as he looked at the doorway. "When did she grow up?"

Hillary sighed and allowed herself to sink back in her chair. "I don't know," she said. "A week ago I wouldn't have believed this possible of her."

"As I remember," he told her, "a week ago, it wasn't."

He shrugged to his feet and, taking her hands, drew her to stand before him.

"Hillary," he said, looking down at her, "I still don't approve."

She saw his resolve in the firm set of his mouth and in the darkness in his eyes.

"She is talented," he said. "None of us can question that. But there has to be another outlet for her."

"Does there, Anton?" Hillary asked. "She loves creating. She loves performing. Why must there be something else?"

"Something else," he insisted, "and some*one* else."

"Why?" There had to be more; Hillary knew there had to be more of a reason than what had happened between them.

There it was again, the look in his eyes that told her she had stepped over the fine boundary he had drawn.

"Does it really matter to you?" he asked. "I'll help her find it. I'll do everything I can to help her. But not with this."

She stiffened and tried to take her hands from his.

She saw the corner of his mouth lift in what in any other situation could almost have been described as a whimsical smile. He released her hands.

"I have to go back to the winery," he said. "Walk me to the porch?"

She dragged a deep breath into her lungs and stared up at him, trying to find strength to say no. But it was no use. She'd go anywhere with him, anytime, and she hated the weakness that made it so.

She nodded and silently followed him onto the front porch. He pulled the massive door shut behind them. They stood in shadows not touched by the bright moonlight—still, quiet—until with one hand he reached out and traced her cheek.

"Did you really treat him just as I treat Constance?" he asked softly.

Hillary sighed, a small sound of both frustration and relief. Maybe he finally, *finally*, understood.

"That's what I've been trying to tell you," she answered just as softly. "He's my little brother. That's all he's ever been. That's all he ever can be to me. And that's all I want from him."

Anton slid his hand from her cheek to her throat and held it there gently.

"Anton . . ." she whispered.

She sensed that he was fighting himself as he bent toward her. But he couldn't win. She knew that. No more than she could win that small battle she had fought just a moment before.

She met his kiss, returned his hunger, returned his need. There was no gentleness in him. His actions spoke too clearly of the doubts and indecisions he still held. But there was no gentleness in Hillary, either. Beneath his touch she became a wild thing, someone she barely recognized. *Take what you can now,* her body cried out to her. *Now, while he still wants you.*

He pulled away from her, looking as dazed as she felt.

"I have to go to the winery," he said raggedly.

Hillary only nodded as she fought to regain her composure.

But he made no move to leave, and she couldn't turn away from him.

"To hell with the winery," he said as he reached for her.

"Hillary . . ."

Her name was a whisper in the air before she surrendered to his arms and his mouth lowered onto hers.

Chapter Nine

Life went on. Daily routines persisted in spite of personal turmoil. It was a lesson Hillary had learned long ago and yet, now, even this deeply ingrained knowledge had the power to surprise her.

She stood on the front porch of the house, watching the activity at the winery—the laden trailers being pulled up to the processing-room doors, the carloads of tourists stopping at the tasting room—and thought that at least someone in that stream of strangers ought to sense the tension building in this peaceful place.

Did Anton love her? As finely tuned as she was to his every word, expression and glance, she couldn't tell. If he did, it was reluctantly, unwillingly. And it was something he would not allow himself to speak of, perhaps not even to think of.

More time. They needed so much more time together. Time for her to show him that he could

trust her. Time for her to nourish his love. Time
to prove hers.

And they didn't have it.

Hillary fought back a flash of resentment against
Tippy and Constance. They were caught, too. But
she couldn't stop the frantic hope that Anton
would not learn about the child until later, much
later, after the marriage was a fact, after he had
accepted Tippy as an enduring part of Constance's
life. Then, perhaps, news of the child would not be
so devastating.

It was a selfish wish. Hillary knew that. But she
couldn't let go of it. She held it to her with a quiet
desperation. Only secrecy, more secrecy could
buy them their time. But at what cost?

Her quiet laugh mocked her. Here she was,
again, trying to build on deception. Would there
ever be an end to it?

ANTON GLANCED UP from his conference with
Frank. Another tour group stood at the doorway,
led by Constance, who knew from experience not
to bring them into the room during harvest. She
spoke quietly, pointing out the first critical steps in
winemaking. Hillary stood at her side.

This was the third time that day he had seen
Hillary with a group. Each time before she had
sought him out with her eyes, asking a silent question he pretended not to understand.

Acknowledgment was what she needed. He
knew that. Acknowledgment from him that the
passion that flared between them was more than a

furtive, momentary thing to be hidden from all who mattered to him. Acknowledgment by a word, a smile or a possessive gesture from him.

Why, he asked himself. Was it only a normal desire from a woman in love? Or was there more? What more evidence could she need that he was trapped in her web as thoroughly—no, damn it— more thoroughly than ever? Acknowledgment, he told himself. Knowing that Constance knew. Knowing that his mother knew.

And he wasn't prepared to give her that, too. Not yet.

He met the question in her eyes with one of his own and watched as she shifted uneasily under his stare. No. He couldn't give her that. Not while she still held something from him. *What is it, Hillary,* he questioned silently. *What other secrets are you hiding behind that innocent face of yours? What other lies are you perpetuating?* A self-deprecatory smile twisted his mouth.

If she knew how much it cost him to stand there silently, to keep himself from pulling her into his arms and damning the consequences, what would she do? Would she surrender with that breathless catch in her voice that drove him nearly crazy with wanting her? Or would she laugh in triumph? Until he knew for sure, he couldn't expose himself any more than he already had. Until he knew for sure, he at least could allow himself the pretense of her love in their stolen moments.

He saw Bill leave his station and amble toward

the tour group. Anton frowned as he watched Bill push his cap back on his head and lean indolently against the door facing, speaking softly yet intensely—to Constance—to Hillary? Anton was too far away to hear the words, but he recognized Bill's actions from watching him in countless flirtations. He started toward him, intending to break up the cozy scene, when he saw Hillary frown, shake her head, and then laugh not quite naturally as Constance urged the group under her direction toward the next stage of the tour.

Damn Bill Roeffler! Anton was stunned by the rage he felt. Didn't Bill have enough women panting after him already? And didn't he have enough to do to keep his thoughts from future conquests at least for the few hours a day Anton paid him to think of winemaking? No wonder his own place had fallen into ruin.

Anton became aware of his fist clenched at his side and forced his body to relax. He already harbored enough resentment against Bill without this. If he were honest with himself, Bill's actions, obnoxious as they were, had not been different enough, or offensive enough, to cause this reaction.

His glance raked over Bill before he forced his expression into one showing only mild frustration.

"Bill."

Bill grinned at him from his perch in the doorway.

Anton nodded toward Bill's untended station.

"Sure, cousin," Bill said, undaunted, as he

walked back toward it. "Just taking a little break. By the way," Bill said, resuming his position as Anton turned away, "do you suppose you could break loose with my check a little early? I've got a small cash problem."

Anton stopped and turned back to Bill. A *small* cash problem? They were in the middle of the best harvest of the last ten years, Bill was sitting on land every bit as rich and potentially as productive as his own, and he had a *small* cash problem? Now might be the time to approach him about buying the land after all.

"Come up to the house after supper," Anton said. "Maybe we can work something out."

IT WAS LIKE A MADHOUSE. In all the days spent at Anton's home, Hillary had never seen crowds like those that descended on the tasting room that afternoon. Where did all the tourists come from? She couldn't envision that many people leaving the speed of interstate travel to visit the sleepy community she had always thought this was. But they did. A cluster of them waited in the corner of the room for yet another tour. Debbie was busy behind the long counter. Karen, another summer employee, cheerfully manned the cash register in retail sales.

Hillary jumped at a tap on her shoulder. "Hillary," Constance said plaintively, "can you take this next tour by yourself? Tippy's supposed to call at three, and if we miss each other this time, I don't know when we'll get to talk."

Hillary shook her head, sympathetic with the pleading in Constance's eyes. "You know I don't know enough to guide a tour," she said. "Maybe it will slow down so that I can fill in for someone else and let Debbie or Karen take the next one."

"And maybe it won't," Constance said as another group of people entered through the front door. "You know enough," she insisted. "You've been through it enough to fake it."

Hillary smiled and glanced at her watch. "We could leave now and maybe..."

"There's no way," Constance said. "Please? Oh, please, Hillary. It's important, or I wouldn't ask."

HILLARY WAS BACK, this time without Constance, and although she gave the outward appearance of calm, Anton recognized potential trouble in the actions of one man in the group she led. The man stepped through the doorway into the processing room.

He was a toucher, Anton thought, a lingerer, a questioner who could take a simple thing like a winery tour and turn it into an inquisition with his ignorant questions and inflated sense of importance.

Anton saw Hillary call the man back to the doorway with a soft word and an apologetic shake of her head. The man hesitated but reluctantly returned to the group.

Why should he worry, Anton thought. Constance had been leading people like that for years.

Hillary must have picked up at least some of her techniques. The worst that could happen was that the tour would run a little longer and be a little more uncomfortable for her.

HILLARY BREATHED A SILENT SIGH as they entered this part of the cellars. Not only was this her favorite part of the tour, it was also the last stage of it. Of the eight people she guided, six seemed genuinely interested in the involved winemaking process from pressing to bottling. Only one, the man on her left, had given her any trouble, and she felt her ignorance must have antagonized him as much as his aggression antagonized her. She had never before said "I don't know" so often in such a short period of time in her life. She felt genuine pity for his wife, who had tried occasionally to question or comment but had been interrupted by him each time.

Hillary gestured toward the dull green bottles racked at an angle in the dark wooden shelves.

"These bottles contain what will be Roeffler's champagne," she said.

"Will be?" the man asked.

"Will be," Hillary told him. "They are racked here until the additional fermenting process is completed." As much as she appreciated the process, she hoped she could remember enough specifics to relate it accurately. "Each day each bottle is given a quarter turn..."

The man reached out and rested his hand on the nearest bottle.

"Oh, please, don't," Hillary said in alarm.

"Why?" he asked. "Is my touch going to contaminate your precious wine?"

"Oh, my God."

Hillary heard the soft whisper of the man's wife. *My sentiments exactly,* she thought, exasperated. But the woman wasn't looking at her husband. She stared to the right, where Anton stood. Framed in a shaft of light from the adjoining room, he was tall and imposing and looked for the first moment very much like the first Anton Roeffler in the faded picture on display in another room in the winery.

"Miss Michaels's concern is for your safety," Anton said softly. "Those bottles are under a great deal of pressure. Occasionally one explodes. We'd hate for you to lose a hand."

The man jerked his hand away and glared at Hillary.

Hillary spoke quickly, happy to share her responsibility. "This is Anton Roeffler," she explained, noticing the women's admiring smiles. "Mr. Roeffler belongs to the fifth generation of vintners who have been making wine in this location for over a hundred years."

The man had not missed his wife's appreciative glances at Anton. "Except, of course, for Prohibition," he said, demanding an admission.

Anton's smile reached only his lips. "Although we concentrated primarily on growing table grapes during that period, it wasn't illegal to make wine," he said, still maintaining a facade of pleasantness, "only to sell it."

"And of course," the man persisted, unwilling to give up center stage, "you didn't sell it."

Hillary watched Anton's jaw clench and then, amazingly, relax. A genuine smile broke across his face as he looked at her. "Actually, we did," he said. "There was a warrant out for my grandfather's arrest for more than a year."

Hillary heard the delighted titters of laughter from the rest of the group.

"Unfortunately, no one could find him to serve the warrant," Anton continued, "and after the repeal of Prohibition, he was pardoned."

Hillary joined in the laughter. Anton had effectively taken control of the situation without rudeness and without any obvious effort.

"Now," he said, "if you'll follow this aisle, it will lead you back to the tasting room, where our staff is waiting to help you sample some of the wines Miss Michaels has been telling you about."

Anton hung back as the group turned.

"Hillary?"

She stepped to one side and waited as the eight tourists walked past her.

"Thank you," she said quietly as he came to her side. "I only thought I knew how much I didn't know."

"You did fine," he said, walking with her as they inobtrusively saw that no one in the group splintered off or lingered behind.

She felt a small start of surprise and then pleasure as Anton draped his arm over her shoulder.

When they reached the door to the tasting room, his arm still rested about her. She glanced at him hesitantly before reaching for the door to join the group.

He pulled her back. "Debbie and Karen can handle it," he said.

She looked up at him. He was searching her face warily, but she couldn't understand what he sought.

"You don't have to work," he said softly. "None of us had any idea you would when Constance asked you to stay."

"I don't mind," she said. "It isn't really like work. It's . . ." Her words trailed off. Would he appreciate hearing that it gave her a chance to be near him? Somehow, she doubted that he would.

She leaned back in his arms and grinned at him. "A bootlegger? Are there any more family skeletons?"

She expected a quick laugh from him in response. Instead, his eyes clouded, and for a moment, although he held her closely, he was far away. He brought himself back to her and smiled gently. "A few," he said.

The tasting room door banged open.

"Hillary—"

Hillary twisted to see Constance just inside the doorway.

"Oh. Hi, Anton."

Constance glanced from her brother to Hillary.

"I thought you were lost," she said finally. "Sorry."

Hillary once again became aware of Anton's arms around her. She looked up at him apologetically. He released her, and she stepped away.

"No," she said. "Not lost."

She forced a bright smile for the unusually silent Constance. "I was just on my way to help."

ALTHOUGH THEY DINED LATE, Anton did not join them for supper that night. Hillary hid her stab of disappointment when she and Constance walked into the kitchen and found the round table set for only three.

Constance, however, did not remain silent. She reached into the freezing compartment, took out the container of ice, and began plunking cubes into the waiting glasses.

"Well, I see we're back to normal," she said. "Big Brother is doing his strong, silent number again, is he?"

"Not quite," Inez answered, but she was facing the refrigerator so Hillary couldn't see her expression. "When he told me he wouldn't be here for supper, I took some sandwiches down to him at the office. He promised he'd be up at a reasonable hour."

Constance grinned then. "By his definition, or yours?"

It was dusk when they finished eating, and almost dark by the time they finished clearing the kitchen and walked to the living room.

A muggy oppression had settled over the hill that afternoon, capturing them in a strength-sapping heat. The windows of the house remained closed, and the air conditioner labored to cool the high-ceilinged rooms.

Hillary glanced toward the living-room windows just in time to see a flash of lightning spear through the sky and to hear the echoing low rumble of thunder. Rain would bring blessed relief from the heat, but she knew what devastation hail, which that storm probably carried, would bring to the harvest now in progress.

"Will you play for us tonight, Constance?" Inez asked as she reached for her knitting.

Hillary smiled. The woman was seldom idle. In the week she had been there, she had watched the afghan in Inez's basket double in size.

"Not tonight, Mom." Constance dropped listlessly into a chair. "It must be the heat. I'm really wrung out. But Hillary might. Would you, Hillary?"

Hillary glanced at her. Was it the heat? Or was Constance not feeling well? She couldn't tell from the young woman's expression.

"Why not?" Hillary said, smiling as she seated herself on the piano bench. "What would you like to hear?"

"How about some blues?" Constance asked. "Something low-down and dirty."

So it wasn't just the heat. But, Hillary realized, it probably wasn't physical discomfort, either, that plunged Constance into this mood. And blues somehow seemed appropriate with the lowering atmosphere outside and with the insecurity that was settling itself around her. Why hadn't Anton come for supper? Was it because Constance had seen him holding her? He had been so careful to hide any sign of involvement with her from his family, and although no one had said anything, Hillary had been aware of Constance's speculative gaze more than once that day.

Hillary glanced at Inez, who smiled pleasantly at her. No, Inez didn't seem to be aware of any of the undercurrents, and she probably wasn't ready for the kind of blues Hillary would play, the kind that clenched at the gut before plummeting to the depth of human emotion. And she, well, Hillary wasn't sure she herself was ready for the honesty of that kind of music, either.

She shook her head. "I think not," she said lightly. "How about some Broadway?"

"Oh, yes," Inez said. "I love the music from *Camelot*."

"*Camelot* it is," Hillary said gently.

For several minutes the only sounds in the room were the occasional click of Inez's knitting needles and the romantic strains of the Broadway score.

Hillary sensed Anton's presence before she saw him, before she heard him. The awareness began as a slow prickle along the back of her neck and grew until it felt as though he were standing just inches from her. Warily she turned her head and saw Anton lounging in the doorway, holding a tall glass of iced tea in his hand. His eyes glittered darkly, and his expression was pulled tautly by a forced smile.

Hillary realized what music she was playing, "If Ever I Should Leave You," and her hands fell silent on the keys.

God, she thought, *was everything she did going to be wrong?*

"Don't stop," he said evenly, saluting her with his glass. "Not because of me."

"Anton." Hillary heard the surprise in Inez's voice, which echoed her own. "You didn't work all night."

"As I recall," he said casually, "you gave me a curfew."

Inez laughed. "Yes, but when did that ever change anything?"

"Well," Constance said, straightening in her chair and at least outwardly shaking off her lethargy, "are you just going to stand there holding up the doorway, or are you going to come in and join us?"

"I'm not sure you want me anywhere near you until I've had a shower," Anton said, still lounging in the doorway. "Sure. Why not?" He pushed away from the door. "It's so nice in here after the oven outside, maybe I will join you. Just for a minute or two."

"Is it going to rain?" Inez asked anxiously.

He shook his head and sprawled into a chair near the piano. He drank deeply from the tea. "I don't think so. It looks as if it's going to stay south of the river." He glanced toward Hillary, and she noticed the slight tightening of his expression. "Don't let me interrupt," he said.

"You're not interrupting," Hillary said softly. "I was almost finished."

"She's taking requests, Anton," Constance said, and Hillary could cheerfully have strangled her. "Don't you have something you want to hear?"

Anton stretched his long legs in front of him and leaned back in the chair. He took another drink from his tea, but his thoughtful gaze remained on her. "Chopin?" he said softly.

Chopin? Was Anton letting the romantic in him surface at last? Hillary wondered if his aversion to musicians' private lives extended to those who had achieved immortality. Probably not. Chopin's life had been as fraught with scandal as any current recording star's. Or was it a test? Comparing her performance with the one Constance had given early the evening before? That thought wiped the beginnings of a smile from Hillary's face.

"Chopin," she said emotionlessly.

He nodded. "I think there's some music in the bench, isn't there Constance?"

It was a test. She faced the piano. Well, she'd never be another Cliburn, or an Ashkenazy, but she certainly had nothing to be ashamed of. Music in the bench indeed!

Mentally she clicked off the selections she knew. Of all of them, one pressed itself forward;

without thinking, she began playing her favorite nocturne. Romantic. Moving. Emotional.

Too late she realized the trap her wounded pride had sprung on her as the lyrics from the popular version drifted through her mind. "To Love Again" it had been renamed.

She felt the quick sting of tears in her eyes and blinked them back. She would not cry in front of him, not again. But as her fingers caressed the keys she could not help thinking bitterly, sure, she had shown him! What she had done was expose herself again. But, damn it, he was the one who had requested Chopin. Maybe he wasn't making the connection between the classical music and the popular. She didn't dare risk a glance at him. This was too blatant a statement. He wasn't yet ready for it. She closed her eyes, remembering what they had once shared, what they could have shared. They did have the right!

She subdued her defiance and frustration, allowing only the beauty of the music to flow into the room, until the last note echoed in the air around them. She sat still and erect, facing the piano, waiting.

"You're very good," Anton said, breaking the silence.

"She ought to be," Constance said enthusiastically. "She trained for the concert stage."

"Oh."

Hillary heard more than one question in Anton's voice.

"My father's dream," Hillary said, still facing the piano. "Not mine."

"And why is that?" Anton asked.

She turned to face him. "I don't like performing."

He raised one eyebrow in disbelief. His smile mocked her. "I would have thought just the opposite."

Yes, Hillary realized, refusing to let herself slump in despair, he would have. Now was not the perfect time, but perhaps it would be the only time she had to explain this one thing to him.

"I never liked being on the stage," she said carefully. "Stage fright is a natural and normal thing, but for me it never ended. If the performance was bad—" she closed her eyes in memory "—it was as though everyone out front was waiting for a mistake, waiting to criticize. And if it was good—I think those were the worst times of all. If I was really living the music, living the emotion of it, it was as though they wanted more, as though they waited to drain me completely."

She opened her eyes to stare into the question in his and saw the doubts waiting there.

When Anton spoke, the doubts were gone, replaced by a bitter mockery. "And feeling as you do, you still insist that this is the right thing for Constance."

"Oh, Anton, for goodness' sake," Constance said from behind her. "It's not the same for everybody. Didn't you hear what she just said?"

Constance stood beside her now, draping an arm over Hillary's shoulder.

"I'm trying to hear what she's saying," Anton said evenly.

"Look," Constance interrupted. "Sure, I have stage fright. The night of the concert in Oklahoma City, I was petrified. But it's worth it!"

She hugged Hillary's shoulder. "Hillary feels they want to devour her. All I feel is the *love*. Do you know..."

Hillary watched Anton's frown deepening as Constance went on, trying to explain.

"... when you're on that stage, and the people *like* what you're doing, there's... there's this wealth of love that just comes from them to you. When they applaud... when they applaud, it makes little ripples in the air that move forward from person to person, until by the time it gets to you on the stage it's like:... it's like..." Constance's free hand went to her cheek. "It's like little pats on the face, little touches of approval. Anton, there's nothing like it."

Anton set his glass of tea on a nearby table and stood. "And is there anything like living on the road, Constance?" he asked as his frown became a scowl. "In a bus? Homeless? Going from town to town? Never knowing where the next job is going to be? Never knowing where your next meal is coming from?"

A smile broke over Constance's face. "Is that what you're worried about?" she asked. "Don't. Sure, it's like that for thousands of people, Anton, and maybe if I ever decide to break out on my own, I'll have some of that. I'm sure we'll be on the road. But I'm not going to starve."

Constance choked back a small laugh. "Anton,

you wouldn't let me starve. I wouldn't let me starve. And Tippy certainly won't let me starve."

Hillary flinched away from the anger she saw in Anton's eyes as he whirled toward his sister.

"And how long do you think that will go on, Constance?" he asked in a clipped voice. "How long do you think it will be before he gets tired of you and moves on to some other plaything? Just how long do you think you will be able to hold on to Tippy Grey?"

Hillary felt Constance shrinking against her and reached for the younger woman's hand.

"Forever," Constance said in a small voice.

"Oh, come on, Constance. You're twenty years old. Sometimes you act like an adult. It's time you started thinking like one."

"I love Tippy," Constance said. "And he loves me."

"For how long?" Anton asked her, relentless in his questioning.

Stop it! Hillary wanted to cry. *Leave her alone!* But something in Anton's eyes, an anguish warring with his anger, kept her from speaking.

"What about when he gets tired of you, Constance?"

"He won't," Constance said.

"He won't? What guarantee do you have of that? You say he wants to marry you. How can you be sure he'll even do that? You deserve better, Constance."

Hillary felt Constance's hand quiver beneath hers and then clench on her shoulder and heard the answering spark of anger in the young woman's voice.

"There isn't anything better," Constance said defiantly. "And what makes you think *I'm* not good enough for *him*?"

"That's not what I said."

"Yes, it is!" Constance took a deep breath. "I'm going to marry him, Anton, and nothing you can say or do will stop me."

"And if I forbid it?"

Don't, Hillary moaned silently. *Don't do this, Anton. Please!*

"You can't," Constance answered.

Hillary saw a quick flash of rage pass across Anton's face before he controlled it. He started to speak, stopped, and turned away, dragging his hand through his hair before he turned back to his sister.

"No, I can't forbid it," he said. He sighed deeply. "A year, Constance. Will you wait a year?"

"No."

"For God's sake, a year isn't forever! If he loves you now, he'll still love you then. And by then you'll have your degree, you'll have some way to support yourself, and you will have a chance to see if this is what you really want or if you're being swept off your feet."

"No."

"Why? That's not so much to ask," he said. "Will you tell me why you won't give me at least that?"

Hillary felt Constance's hand sliding from her

shoulder, felt the young woman stiffen. *Oh, no,* she thought, *please don't,* knowing that her wish was an impossible one, knowing that her time had run out. She heard the words from a distance, blurred by the rush of grief that filled her. Inevitable. It had all been inevitable.

"Because it's not my year to give you," Constance said. Hillary heard the catch in her voice before she continued. "I'm pregnant."

Chapter Ten

Hillary heard Inez's sharp intake of breath, Constance's labored breathing, her own heartbeat and another low rumble of thunder, but she saw only the swift progression of emotions crossing Anton's face—stunned comprehension, disbelief, anger, pain and finally—resignation?

Infinitely gentle, infinitely sad, he reached to touch Constance, but she shrugged away from him. He let his arm drop to his side.

He turned to Hillary. Her breath caught and refused to move when she saw the bleakness in his eyes.

"You knew."

She wanted to deny it, wished to God she could deny it, but she couldn't.

She watched life creep back into him—a cold, glittering rage.

"All this time you knew."

She forced herself to breathe, but she could not move or speak.

"Are you happy now? Do you finally have what you want?"

What Hillary wanted was to cry out against his accusations, but all she could do was drag her head from side to side in denial.

"Why?"

But she heard no question, only condemnation, in his voice.

"'I didn't know, Anton,'" he said bitterly. "'Didn't know they were involved.'" His harsh laugh cut through her. "And you only agreed to stay here because of concern for Constance."

"Leave her alone!" Constance cried. "Yell at me if you have to. *I'm* the one who's pregnant. Why are you attacking Hillary?"

"You've been used, Constance," he said in a monotone. "We all have been. What I don't know is why." His eyes dismissed her answer as he asked again, "Why, Hillary?"

Trust her? Hillary fought back a hysterical need to laugh. She had actually thought this man could trust her? Could love her?

"What are you talking about?" Constance asked.

"She introduced you," Anton told her. "She encouraged you. And she made sure she was here when we found out. Isn't that right, Hillary?"

Each statement was true, but added together, as Anton had added them, they presented such a different picture of what had actually happened, of her motives, that Hillary couldn't answer.

"What game are you playing now?"

"No game," Hillary finally whispered. "None of this has ever been a game."

Constance spoke then, not shamed as Hillary would have thought, not frightened and definitely not docile. "Will you please tell me what's going on?"

"Ask your friend," Anton told her. "Ask your good friend Hillary. Will you tell her?" he asked Hillary. "Or do you want me to?"

Hillary looked from the disgust in his eyes to Inez, who sat in stunned silence with tears spilling over her cheeks, to Constance, whose stance and expression demanded an answer. She regretted the twinge of jealousy she had felt—was it really only the day before?—for Constance's confidence in Tippy's love. Maybe that confidence would carry her through this. Hillary hoped it was strong enough for Constance to place the old rumors in their proper perspective, to see them for what they were, merely old rumors.

Hillary twisted to face Constance, but she was not strong enough yet to rise. Silently she pleaded with the young woman to understand. Constance's clear gray eyes held such trust that for a moment Hillary couldn't force herself to speak. She felt Anton move beside her. If she didn't tell her, he would. She found her voice.

"I'm ... I was ..." Hillary took a deep breath. There was nothing to do but to say it. "I'm Rhee Weston."

Hillary watched confusion cloud Constance's face. From the doorway came a sharp sound, and then another—deliberate, denigrating applause from one person. She felt Anton's jolt of surprise as she turned to the sound.

Bill stood in the doorway.

"That was a beautiful performance," Bill said. "Even to the trembling lower lip. You missed your calling. You should never have tried to be a singer. Acting is your field."

"What the hell are you doing here?"

"Why, cousin, you invited me. Don't you remember? When no one answered my knock, I came on in."

Hillary forced herself to stand. An actress? Maybe she should have been one, because while every nerve in her body protested moving, protested doing anything other than huddling in abject misery, she was able to straighten her shoulders, to toss back her head, to glare icily across the room. She didn't doubt that she owed Constance and Inez an explanation, but she owed Bill Roeffler nothing.

Hillary stopped in front of Inez's chair. Inez looked up at her. Hillary saw still more tears in the woman's eyes, and an anguish far deeper than even the news divulged tonight could possibly warrant.

Hillary started to speak and then realized she had nothing that she could say to this woman.

She turned, brushed past Bill as she left the room, and started up the stairs.

"Hillary, wait!" she heard Constance call, and then a muffled oath. "Get your hands off me,

Bill," she heard Constance say. "You may have been invited, but you're certainly not welcome now, and nothing that's going on has anything to do with you."

Hillary reached her room by the time she heard Constance's steps running up the stairs. Quietly she closed the door behind her, crossed the room, and reached for her suitcase. She laid it across the bed just as the door crashed open.

"Will you please tell me what's going on," Constance said breathlessly.

Hillary rested her hands, palms down, on the suitcase, and slumped in defeat before turning to face Constance. Her voice caught in her dry throat as she forced herself to speak carefully.

"If you don't believe anything I say ever again, Constance," she said slowly, "believe this. The rumors were not true."

"I know."

Hillary blinked. "You know?"

"Of course I know. I asked Tippy about them months ago, when I first recognized you."

Hillary groped for the support of the bed and lowered herself to it.

"But you never said anything."

Constance smiled at her and shook her head. "Tippy told me how the university felt about Rhee Weston, and how you guarded your privacy. I'll admit it was a shock when it first dawned on me who you were. I'd been a Tippy Grey fan for years. I had every magazine I could find with anything about him in it." Constance laughed disparagingly. "I used to be really jealous of you, but it wasn't you, Hillary, it was . . . it was that woman in the . . . in the pictures, and by the time I associated you with her, I knew you."

Hillary felt one tear escape and trickle down her cheek. *Trust.* Constance gave it so freely.

Constance crossed the room and knelt in front of her, taking Hillary's hands in her own. "What I don't understand," she said, "is how Anton knows, and why it makes such a difference to him."

"Connie . . ." Hillary freed one hand and brushed dark hair away from the younger woman's forehead. She had a right to know. So much of what had happened was because of it. "The summer I disappeared . . ."

"Yes?" Constance prompted.

Hillary drew a deep breath and continued. "The summer I was missing, I was here."

She watched the surprise in Constance's eyes, but Constance remained silent.

"Here. Not actually at the winery. I had a room and a job in Ozark. Anton helped me find them. He didn't know who I was."

"But why didn't I know?" Constance asked.

Hillary smiled tremulously. "That was the summer your brother Timothy's wife broke her leg. You and your mother were in Little Rock. But I knew about you. I saw your picture."

Too easily Hillary was trapped in memories of happier days, days of exploring each other, learning about each other—almost.

"Anton didn't know who I was," she repeated. "I couldn't... didn't even tell him my real name. And I isolated myself from news broadcasts, from anything remotely resembling the outside world. He was with me when I saw the newscast talking about my death. He had just asked me to marry him."

"Oh, Lord," Constance whispered and tightened her hand on Hillary's.

"And he took me to the airport to meet the plane Tippy sent after me."

For the second time that evening, Hillary watched a progression of emotions play across someone's face. Constance remained on her knees, silent. When she spoke, she spoke gently. "He loved you."

"Yes," Hillary said.

"And you? Did you love him?"

"Yes."

"That explains it then," Constance said softly. "I couldn't imagine what was wrong with him, why he was treating you the way he was. Do you still love him?"

"I don't think that matters now," Hillary said.

"Not matter?" Constance jumped to her feet and paced the room. "Of course it matters. If that pea-brained, bullheaded brother of mine had the sense God gave a... a grape, he'd..."

Constance whirled to face her. "Hillary, I'm sorry. I had no idea what I was putting you through. I would never have insisted you stay if I had known. I would..."

Constance raked her hand through her hair in a gesture so similar to Anton's that Hillary caught her breath at the resemblance between the two of them.

"If I'd known," Constance continued, "I would have done everything differently."

Hillary shook her head. "No, Constance. I'm the one who's sorry. If it hadn't been for me, maybe you and Tippy wouldn't have had to tiptoe around Anton's emotions so much. Maybe you could have been more open."

"That's pure, unadulterated bull," Constance said. "Oh, yes, I'm sure it has something to do with his attitude toward Tippy personally, but not…not…" She shook her head. "I don't know how far back it goes, but as long as I can remember, I've had to hide any interest I had in popular music from the family, Anton and Mother both. What happened between you and Anton may have reinforced his feelings, but it wasn't the beginning of them, and I won't let you take the blame for it."

"Are you sure, Constance? I've gone through hell thinking this was all my fault."

"I'm sure," Constance said. "Now, answer my question." Her voice softened. "Do you still love him?"

Hillary glanced down at her hands, clasped loosely in her lap. Slowly she straightened her fingers and smoothed the denim of her jeans across her thighs. What harm could it do now to admit this much? "Yes."

"And what are you going to do about it?"

Hillary glanced up. "Do?"

"Do," Constance said.

"I don't think there's anything I can do," Hillary told her. "I had thought . . . I had hoped . . ." She smiled wryly at the memory of all she had hoped for. "I had hoped that he would . . . that I would be able to show him what kind of person I really am. I'm not so very different from the woman he fell in love with. I had even thought I was making some progress. But not tonight, Constance. Tonight showed me how wrong I was. He's never going to be able to forgive me for lying. Never."

"So you're just going to pack up and leave?"

"I don't see any alternative."

"Good grief, Hillary, if you go now, you'll only reinforce his feelings, and he's so damned stubborn I'm not sure he'll ever come to you. He cares for you."

"Sure he does."

"No. No, he has to. I've seen him look at you when you didn't know he was watching, when he didn't know *I* was watching, and I thought I must be imagining what I saw, because his attitude was so completely different, but now it all fits together. Don't leave, not yet. Give it a few more days." Her voice and her eyes pleaded with Hillary. "My brother really is a wonderful person when he's not being defensive, and as hard as he's defending himself now, there have to be some pretty serious feelings involved."

Hillary smiled up at her. "You're a dreamer, Constance, and an incurable romantic."

"Maybe," Constance said, "but I don't think that's such a bad thing to be. Please, Hillary. Stay?"

Stay. Hillary wanted to. She was almost afraid to admit, even to herself, how much she wanted to do just that. But not to face the Anton she had seen tonight. But perversely, she didn't want that to be the last memory she had of him, either.

Could Constance be right? Part of what she said echoed impressions Hillary had begun to accept. If Anton was really defending himself against his feelings for her, there could be hope. She knew she wasn't the person he had built her into, and Constance, thank God, knew it also. It was only a matter of convincing Anton. *Only* a matter of convincing Anton? Right now that was the biggest "only" in the world. She thought she had made some progress, until tonight, and maybe she had. Maybe his reaction tonight was founded completely in his shock at the news. Maybe. *Maybe. Maybe. Maybe.* There were so many maybes. But she would never know if she left now.

She looked up at Constance and nodded in acquiescence.

Constance ran to her and threw her arms around her in a hug. "Hillary, you won't be sorry."

Hillary managed to grin as she returned the young woman's hug, disentangled herself, stood and replaced the suitcase.

"I wish I could be as sure of that as you are."

The memory of that last confrontation in the living room flashed through her mind, bringing to her a clear picture of Inez's grief-filled eyes—Inez, who had not said one word. Hillary's grin slid away.

"Constance, your mother needs you."

Constance's smile faded, too, at the words. "I know," she said. "Hillary, I never wanted to hurt her. She's given me so much."

Hillary put her hand on Constance's shoulder and then grabbed her in a quick, comforting hug. "Then why don't you tell her?"

GETTING RID OF BILL tactfully was not easy. As a member of the family, he had come and gone in the Roeffler household at will since childhood, and now he seemed to feel he had a right to intrude in this very private moment.

Anton eased him toward the front door with a promise to talk to him at the winery the next day, wanting at that moment simply to throw him out of the house and knowing that there were too many valid reasons why he couldn't.

Anton finally closed the door on Bill, turned and leaned against it, gathering strength and seeking the calm he knew his mother would need. Later he could sort out his own thoughts. Later he could deal with this newest betrayal. He clenched his hand into a fist and beat once against the door.

Had he believed what he said to her? He must have. The words had come too easily, unbidden, without thought. *Not now!* He couldn't afford to let himself think about her now. He pushed away from the door and returned to the living room.

Inez still sat in the chair with her forgotten knitting spilling over her lap. He walked to her and knelt in front of her, reaching for her hands.

"Mom."

His mother looked at him through tear-filled eyes.

"Anton," she said. "Hillary is... Hillary is the woman, isn't she?"

He closed his eyes and nodded.

"I'm sorry. Do you... does it..."

"It's all right, Mom," he told her. "Right now what we have to think about is Constance."

"Oh, Anton." Her voice broke on a sob. "It's happening, isn't it? In spite of all we did, it's happening."

"No," he said. "It isn't. I won't let it. I promise you that."

He heard footsteps approaching and rose to his feet, clasping her hand one more time before he moved to her side. He looked toward the doorway. Constance and Hillary stood there. Constance was looking at her mother. Hillary was trying not to look at him.

"Mom?" Constance said hesitantly.

Inez looked up at Constance and started to rise.

"Oh, Mom," Constance cried, running to her. "I didn't mean to hurt you. I never wanted to hurt you."

Anton captured Hillary's gaze and saw the glimmer of unshed tears sparkling in her eyes. She didn't look away from him. At least, he thought, there was no sign of the triumph he had expected to see in her expression. But other than that, he read nothing to tell him what she was thinking, or what she was feeling.

He tore his gaze away from her and looked at Constance, now clasped in his mother's arms. What had Hillary told her? Had she told her the truth? The two had returned to the room together.

For a moment he fought the urge to drag Hillary from the house with him and demand explanations from her, and then, because he was losing his control and thought he might do just that, he turned and strode from the room. He slammed the front door behind him as he escaped into the night.

The night air swathed him in its oppressiveness. He had no idea where he was going, only wanting to get away from the scene in the living room. He glanced toward the now-dark winery. The cellars would at least be cool—and a reminder of how far he had come in the past fifteen years since taking over after his father's death. Not far, he admitted silently. Not in what mattered.

What were some of the terms people had used to describe him after they had stopped waiting for him to fail? Innovative. Farseeing. He smiled bitterly. One banker had eventually gone so far as to use the term "brilliant."

But if he were so damned brilliant, why did he feel as impotent now as he had felt at fifteen?

From his determined walk as he strode toward the fields, anyone watching would think he knew where he was going—and once he had known. Once it had seemed so clear-cut. Restore the vineyards. Restore the winery. And then build them to the potential he knew was there. And while doing it, provide a home for his mother. Make up to her for the abuses and pain his father had caused her. And make a home for Constance.

Once that had been enough, more than enough. Until Hillary had come, showing him there could be more in his life than just work. Showing him how much love he had locked inside him, wanting to share.

Damn her for this latest deception! No, he thought, *damn him.* He'd had more than adequate warning; when she left, and again when he found out who Constance was staying with, but like a mistreated dog he'd had to go back and get kicked again. And that was his fault.

If he were the only one involved, he might be able to understand his blindness when it came to Hillary, but Constance's future was at stake, and his mother's happiness. They were the victims, and the child.

He stopped in his mindless march. The child.

He stood alone in the middle of acres of neat rows of vines, head bowed in defeat, as he acknowledged the one thing he had tried to deny all evening. He still wanted her. He still wanted to twist what he knew were facts to fit what she had told him. He still wanted to believe her.

"Damn you, Hillary," he whispered. "Why do you do it? And how do you do it?" Knowing her, knowing her lies, trusting her in anything would be tantamount to surrendering his own powers of reasoning.

I loved you Anton. I never stopped loving you. He heard her words, but was it memory or desire? What kind of fool was he, because even now he wanted to believe them.

Was there any way she could convince him that she meant those words? Would she even want to, now?

The house was dark when he returned. Silently he let himself in and just as silently climbed the stairs. At the top, he stopped and looked, against his will, toward her door. Was she asleep? He realized where his thoughts were leading, where the urgings of his body were leading. He uttered a short, descriptive curse and turned toward his own room.

HILLARY HEARD THE DOOR at the other end of the hall open and then close. She twisted on her side and pressed a hand to her mouth to stifle her low moan. She hadn't really expected him to come to her tonight, but the finality of that door closing forced her to admit that she had hoped.

Hoped what? she asked herself. *That he would make love to you? That he would talk to you? That he would say he understood?*

Yes! All of it, she admitted.

The emptiness inside her was a physical thing,

an ache growing more intense with each passing moment. Would she never be free of it?

She could go to him. That thought flitted through her mind and then lodged. She could go to him. The worst he could do would be to ask her to leave.

No, she realized. The worst he could do, feeling as he now felt, would be to ask her to stay.

She grabbed the other pillow and hugged it close to her. She had swallowed her pride when Constance asked her earlier not to leave, because in spite of all that had happened, she still didn't think there was much room for pride when one loved someone as much as she loved Anton. But still, some pride was necessary.

That pride kept her from leaving her room, from going to him. But that pride and the pillow were poor substitutes for Anton's warm, loving body holding her close through the sleepless night.

Chapter Eleven

Hillary sat at the dressing table, elbows propped on its smooth dark surface, resting her face against both fists as she tried to find the energy to finish dressing. It had been early morning when she finally fell asleep. The last thing she remembered was listening to the calls of awakening birds and watching the light in the room change to a pale gray. Too soon, the sounds of harvesters arriving with still more grapes had dragged her from that sleep.

She grimaced at her reflection in the mirror as she heard a light tap at the door and prepared herself for Constance's lecture.

"Come in," she mumbled.

Constance stuck her head around the partially opened door, looked at Hillary and then came on into the room. Without saying anything, she walked to the dressing table, picked up the compact of blusher and handed it to Hillary.

Hillary chuckled. "Thanks a lot. You're a true friend and morale-booster."

"Oh, anytime," Constance said. "But if it's any consolation, I had to resort to that myself this morning."

Hillary took the compact but didn't open it. She looked up at the young woman.

"What am I doing here, Constance? I've got to be out of my mind to stay."

"No," Constance said, "don't say that. Everything's going to be all right. For both of us."

ANTON WAS NOT IN THE BEST OF MOODS. He had spent two hours in the field coaxing a recalcitrant automatic picker back into operation. He'd returned to find Frank Huddleston muttering dire threats and waving a wrench at the new must pump, and then a high-pressure hose had broken loose while Frank's son, Wayne, was rinsing down one of the new stainless-steel fermenting tanks, drenching three people to the extent that they had to go home to change clothes.

No, he admitted to himself as he closeted himself in his office with the day's mail, he was not in a very good mood at all.

When he had chosen winemaking, or it had chosen him, he had envisioned modernizing the winery. What he hadn't envisioned were the changes that just a few years could make. Now he found he had to be mechanic, chemist and even psychologist in dealing with personnel problems. And that, he admitted, scowling, was not the problem, either.

He slumped back in his chair. Everyone else

had been asleep when he left the house that morning. He hadn't yet talked to Constance. He didn't, in all honesty, know what he was going to say to her when he did.

Times had changed. There was no longer quite so much stigma attached to bearing a child out of wedlock as there had been twenty years before, but in this closely knit community there could be little chance of hiding it.

There were options. His brother Ben would welcome her into his home in Fort Smith, Timothy into his home in Little Rock. She wouldn't have to stay here and face the questions. No, at least those would be delayed for a while. And she would have her family's support. That much he could be sure of.

And as for Tippy Grey... He felt his hands clenching and forced them to relax. She'd get over him. He knew Constance thought she was in love with Tippy, but at twenty... at twenty a girl could believe a lot of things.

The sharp rap on his office door was an unwanted intrusion. Anton glanced up, wondering what new emergency had arisen as the door opened and Bill walked in.

"Are you ready to talk to me?"

No, he wasn't. But he had put Bill off twice already.

"All right," Anton said. "Come on in. Have a chair."

He reached automatically for his checkbook. After all, that was what Bill had asked for. Anton completed the check except for his signature and looked across the desk. He was in the wrong frame of mind for this, but maybe Bill wasn't.

"What do you intend to do with your land?" Anton asked.

"Do with it?" Bill said. "I thought I was doing just fine with it as it is."

Yes, he would think that.

"You know, Bill, land can sometimes be a responsibility tying a person to a place where he really doesn't want to be. From watching you over the past few years, I wonder if that's not your case."

Anton saw the flash of interest in Bill's eyes before he masked it and settled more comfortably in the chair.

"It's home, Anton," he said. "The only home I've known."

Anton tore the check from the book and held it on the desk in front of him.

"This is an advance for a week's work, Bill. I don't know what you're going to do with it or why you need it. It doesn't really matter. But unless you do something, and do it quickly, you're always going to be needing an advance on another week's work. I can as easily write you your ticket out of that as I can sign this check."

Bill glanced from the check to Anton's eyes. "And why would you do that?"

"For the Roeffler land," Anton said. "To erase the years of misuse and neglect. To make it as productive as it can be."

"And *I* can't do that?" Bill asked.

"You haven't. And I don't see any indication that you intend to. I haven't even seen any indication that you want to."

Bill grinned, but there was a speculative gleam in his eyes. "It's where I live. How I support myself. What would I do without it?"

Anton fought back a flash of annoyance. "With the money we're talking about, finding a place to live won't be a problem. Getting established in something else won't be a problem."

"But all I know is the vineyard."

No, Anton thought. Bill didn't even know the vineyard. If he knew that, he'd have one instead of a few acres of table grapes.

"You want to put it back together, don't you?" Bill asked. "You can't stand seeing Roeffler land lying idle. What will you do with the house? Bulldoze it down?"

"I don't know," Anton told him. "I hadn't thought about that. It would be a shame to."

"Is that all you can say?" Bill asked. "That it would be a *shame* to destroy the home I was born in, that my father was born in? Oh, yeah. That would be a shame. But that would be one way of getting rid of the poor relation, wouldn't it?"

It was an act, Anton realized as he watched Bill. There was no genuine anger in the man. It was merely a bargaining technique. Maybe he wasn't handling this so badly after all.

"What if I don't want to be pushed out?" Bill

asked. "What if I want to remain here, living in my home, growing my grapes?"

Anton picked up his pen, signed his name to the check, and pushed it across the desk to Bill, but he didn't release it.

"All right. Here's my offer. I buy the land, except for the house and the vineyards you have now. Think about it. But not for too long."

He released the check, closed his checkbook, put it in his desk drawer, stood up and left the office.

HILLARY HELPED CONSTANCE in the tasting room—the activity there was much preferable to the solitude of the house—although she steadfastly refused to help with any tours, not wanting, just yet, to run the risk of any confrontation with Anton.

A new tour group was being formed when the telephone rang. Hillary watched Constance answer the telephone, put the call on hold and hurry to a back office to take the call.

Tippy, Hillary thought. When Constance returned to the tasting room, her eyes were unnaturally bright, and Hillary suspected that she was close to tears.

"Tippy sends his love," Constance said softly.

"You didn't tell him?"

"No. No, what could he do about it besides worry?"

"Constance..."

"Later, Hillary."

Constance pasted a bright smile on her face and

approached the waiting group. "All right, ladies and gentlemen, please come with me."

HILLARY WONDERED how many crises Inez had weathered by going automatically through her daily routines, forcing herself to complete long-established patterns rather than giving way to the grief that filled her.

Several, Hillary decided, watching the woman's restrained actions as she snapped a clean white tablecloth across the round table in the kitchen and smoothed it into place.

Except for her silent tears the night before and that one moment when Constance ran to her, Hillary had not seen Inez's composure crack since the day of her arrival, but she sensed a brittleness in the woman's competent movements and a strength she had only suspected before.

But how much of it was strength, she wondered, and how much of it an ability to avoid facing what was really happening?

Constance burst into the kitchen still flushed and glowing from her bath.

"Sorry I'm late," she said, reaching for a stack of plates. "I guess I was more tired than I thought." She chuckled. "I fell asleep in the tub."

Inez took the plates from her and smiled briefly before turning to the table. "That's all right, Constance. Just sit down. Hillary's been helping. Besides, you need to slow down now."

Constance's flush grew even brighter. She

dropped into a nearby chair. She nibbled at her lower lip and then glanced up at Inez.

"Like you did, Mom? I've heard the stories about how you worked in the fields and in the winery."

"That was then," Inez said. She opened the refrigerator, took out a half gallon of milk, poured a large glassful of it and set it in front of Constance. "Then it was necessary. Now it isn't."

Anton joined them for supper, a silent meal. *What am I doing here?* Hillary wondered as she had countless times through the day. *I don't belong here. I'm not wanted. I can't do any good by staying.*

Inez cleared the table, waving away Hillary's hesitant offer to help. She refilled the iced-tea glasses and then sat down.

"Constance," Anton said finally, obviously uncomfortable with what he was going to say, and just as obviously determined to say it, "we have to talk."

That's my exit line if I ever heard one, Hillary thought. She folded her napkin and placed it on the table. "If you'll excuse me..."

"No!" Constance said, reaching for Hillary's hand. "No," she whispered. "Please stay."

Hillary saw the scathing look Anton cast toward Constance's hand resting on hers. She watched as the lines of his face etched themselves into a grim smile. He would not meet her eyes, but he nodded. She settled herself uneasily into the chair and waited.

"All of us acted on emotion last night, Constance," he continued reluctantly, "without thinking of the consequences of what we said. Your news was a shock. There's no point in denying it. It was painful and disappointing. And there's no point in denying that, either."

Hillary saw Constance flinch and shoot an icy glare toward Anton.

"Painful and disappointing," he repeated, "but not for the reasons you think."

Hillary watched the grim lines of Anton's face soften as he looked at his sister. "We love you, Constance," he said. "Nothing you could ever do will change that. And our love is not conditional. It doesn't demand that we approve of all your actions, just that we accept who you are. Constance—" his voice lowered as he leaned forward "—you have put yourself in a position to be hurt, terribly hurt, and I'm not sure you fully understand the responsibility you have burdened yourself with. That's why we were disappointed—*for* you, not *with* you—and that's why it's painful. Because of what it can mean to you."

Whatever reply Constance would have made was silenced by the loud rap on the back door.

"Oh, hell!" Anton muttered, swiveling toward the door. "What is it now?"

The door swung open, and without waiting for anyone to invite him in, Bill entered the room.

Anton fixed on him a gaze filled with barely contained fury before controlling his features. His voice only hinted at his anger. "Can it wait?"

Bill surveyed the four of them sitting tensely at

the table. A slow grin crossed his face before he closed the door.

"Maybe," he said, "but from the looks of things, it's right on point."

He pulled an extra chair up to the table and straddled it, resting his arms on its back as he devoted his attention to Anton.

"I've been thinking about our talk this morning, and about your problem."

"No, it's not on point, Bill," Anton said, interrupting him.

"Sure it is. You're right. The Roeffler land should be reunited. It should never have been divided. But I don't think just selling it to you is the way to go. The family should be reunited, too. There's only one way to accomplish that. I'll marry Constance."

Constance's short splutter of laughter broke the silence that fell in the room. Hillary turned toward her.

"Marry me?" Constance said. "You?"

Hillary watched the younger woman's humor fade and her face blanch.

"You're serious, aren't you, Bill?" Constance whispered. Bill only nodded. "How dare you?" Constance asked in a hushed voice, overturning her chair as she scrambled from the table. "Anton, how dare you discuss me with . . . with *him*!"

"Constance, wait!" Anton said, rising, reaching to stop her in her flight from the room.

"No!" She scooted past him, only pausing when she reached the safety of the doorway. "I've waited all I'm going to. I've listened all I'm going to. I really thought you loved me. I really thought you were acting this way because you cared! Buy your precious land," she screamed at him, "but I'll be damned before I'll let you use me for barter!"

"Constance!" Anton's voice was a frustrated growl as he called after her.

Hillary was on her feet, moving toward the door, as Constance fled from the room. Anton's solid back filled her path. She pushed past him. He caught her arm and whirled her to face him. Only fleetingly did she notice the bleakness in his eyes.

"Let go of me," she said with venomous softness.

"Hillary . . ."

She wrenched her arm from his grasp and ran after Constance.

Anton listened to the receding sounds of their steps, knowing that even if he followed, neither was likely to listen to him. Not now, at least.

"Damn!"

He doubled his fist and beat in frustration against the door facing before turning his attention back to Bill.

"What in the hell gave you the idea I would let you anywhere near Constance, much less even consider a marriage between the two of you?"

Bill's grin faded a little, but he spoke calmly. "You want the land. You can't stand Tippy Grey. You don't have a whole lot of other options."

Anton's fist was still clenched. He stretched it

open and stuffed his hands in his pockets, fighting the urge to substitute Bill's face for the door facing.

"If you say one more word, Bill," he said tightly, "you're going to be looking for a new job and a new market for your grapes. I'll pay you for the land, but only with money, and the longer you wait, the less money that's going to be."

"It's time for you to leave now, Bill," Inez said quietly.

Anton turned in surprise toward his mother. She sat proudly straight in her chair, and her eyes sparkled dangerously with a light he had thought never to see in them again.

"Anton runs the winery. If he chooses not to fire you because of this, I won't interfere. But he may have a problem, because I promise you, Bill Roeffler, if I hear one word about this or about Constance from anyone, *anyone*, you will not step foot on this property again as long as I live. Is that clear?"

Bill's mouth gaped open. He tried to hold on to his bravado, but it slipped badly.

"Close the door behind you, Bill," Inez said in the same soft voice.

Bill looked to Anton, who only nodded toward the kitchen door.

When the door slammed behind Bill, Anton walked to his mother. He knelt down, giving her a quick, fierce hug as he kissed her cheek.

"Welcome back," he said gently. "I didn't think I was ever going to see the fire in you again."

She laughed self-consciously. "I'm so tired of running scared," she said. "I'm so tired of feeling guilty. Besides, two of my children need me."

He shook his head in quick denial. His mother smiled at him and touched his cheek. "All right," she said. "I won't argue with you now. Now we have to think about Constance."

HILLARY FOLLOWED CONSTANCE to her attic bedroom. Constance had already thrown a suitcase on the bed and was tossing clothes into it, sniffling as tears ran down her cheeks.

Hillary sat on the bed and watched silently, gathering her thoughts, trying to decide what to say, when the memory of a similar scene struck her.

"I wonder what's going to wear out first," she said, "our luggage or our clothes."

Constance stopped in her march to the closet and turned toward her.

"Oh, Hillary!" she wailed as she threw herself into Hillary's arms. "I'm not going to marry that awful man. No one can make me!"

"Sshh," Hillary murmured, holding Constance close. "Of course you're not. And no one can make you, Connie. No one! You know that. Your family knows that."

"Then why—" Constance's voice broke "—Hillary, he tried to *sell* me!"

Four years earlier, a week earlier, even the day before, Hillary would have denied that statement, swearing that Anton loved Constance too much even to consider such a thing. Now...now, although she wanted to comfort Constance, the words of denial wouldn't come.

"Don't be too sure." It was all she could say. "Sometimes...sometimes things aren't the way they seem."

"You heard him, Hillary!" Constance mimicked Bill's words: "'I've been thinking about our talk this morning and about your problem.' What else could it be? It's the land Anton loves. Oh, how could I have been so blind? It's always been the land. Never me! Never me." She drew away from Hillary. "He didn't deny it."

No, Hillary remembered, Anton hadn't denied it. He and Inez had been silent until after Constance's outburst, as silent as she had been. Only her silence had been caused by shock. And theirs? No. It was too pat. Even given Bill's deviousness, the entire scheme fit Anton's feelings too well. It was a nice, tidy way of protecting Constance from his imagined evils of Tippy and getting something he wanted at the same time.

But it was so different from the Anton she had known before, the Anton whose eyes glowed, whose smile softened, whose voice throbbed with pride when he talked about his little sister.

"I'm calling Tippy," Constance said. "I'm not staying here another night." Her laugh bordered on hysteria. "I believed them, Hillary. I wanted so much to believe them. But they're not going to approve of my marriage to him, not ever, and it's not going to do any good to stay around. How could Anton do this to me? Oh, how could he do it?"

Knowing that she could never be objective, Hillary forced herself at least to be calm. "He hasn't done anything yet, Constance. Please. Don't... don't judge him until you've talked with him. And for God's sake, don't call Tippy while you're in this mood. You wouldn't even tell him they knew you were pregnant because it would worry him. What do you think this kind of news will do?"

Constance sniffed and looked up at her. "He'd come for me. He would."

Hillary smiled sadly. "In a minute, Constance. Don't ever doubt that. But do you have any idea what would happen if you sent for him now? With emotions as tightly strung as they are, with tempers as volatile as they are, either he or Anton would be hurt, and you don't want that, not really, because as angry as you are right now, you still love your brother and your mother. If you didn't, you wouldn't feel so betrayed, would you?"

Constance snatched a tissue from the box beside the bed and swiped angrily at her eyes. She leaned against the dresser and distractedly began shredding the tissue. She took a long, steadying breath and looked at Hillary. "He probably thinks it's best for me. Why does he have to be so damned stubborn?"

Hillary shook her head. That was a question she couldn't answer. "I don't know, Constance, and I don't guess I ever will, but..." She ventured a tentative smile. "This is one thing he's going to have to be convinced he's wrong about."

She rose from the bed and held out her hand for Constance. "And neither hysterics nor running away will do that."

"Oh, Hillary." Constance clutched at her hand. "I'm so sorry. You shouldn't have to be in the middle of this."

Hillary returned the pressure of the young woman's hand. She agreed with that statement completely. "Neither should you, Constance. But we both are, and it's time we did something about it."

WHEN THEY REACHED THE KITCHEN DOOR, Hillary put her arm over Constance's shoulder, giving her a reassuring hug and then a gentle push.

Inez was still seated at the kitchen table. Anton leaned against the cabinet. Inez smiled hesitantly. Anton remained expressionless.

Constance looked around the kitchen. "Where's Bill?"

"It's just an educated guess," Anton said, "but by now he's had time to get to a bar and he should be about finished with his first beer."

"I'm not marrying Bill," Constance said. "Neither of you can make me do it. I'm marrying Tippy just as soon as we can get a license."

"Damn it, Constance!" Anton pushed himself away from the cabinet.

"No! No, Anton. We would have been married

already if I hadn't let you bring me home, and then this scene would never have had to take place. But I wanted to listen to you. I've listened all I'm going to. What gives you the right to run roughshod over my life?"

"Constance."

Hillary heard his anger and frustration in the softly spoken word.

"I'm not trying to run your life. I'm trying to save you from being hurt."

It was a broken record playing over and over and over, and Hillary was so tired of hearing it.

"Save her from being hurt?" she said. "Is that what you're really doing? Saving her from marrying a young man whom she loves, a young man who loves her. Oh, Anton, I don't think so. What on earth is so wrong with two young people loving each other? What do you need to save her from? And how are you saving her by pushing her into a marriage with no love at all? And just in case you don't know what one of those can be like, let me tell you—"

"Stop it." Inez pushed her chair back and rose from the table. "All of you."

Hillary turned in surprise.

The older woman walked to Constance, stopped in front of her and stood watching her for a moment. She reached to brush a lock of hair from Constance's forehead.

"No one is going to force you to marry anyone you don't want to marry," Inez said softly.

Hillary watched a quiver cross Constance's

mouth and saw the sparkle of still more tears, but Constance held herself erect and defiant.

"And the rest of it, Mom?" she asked. "You never planned to agree to my marriage to Tippy, did you?"

Inez dropped her hand to her side. "No, I didn't. But..."

Constance shook her head. "Never mind." She took a step backward. "I don't think we have anything else to talk about."

She spun on her heel. Anton stopped her as she reached the door.

"Where are you going?"

Constance looked from him to Hillary, then back to Anton. Her shoulders slumped in defeat.

"Just upstairs, Big Brother. Where else would I go right now?"

She stared pointedly at his hand on her arm until he released her, stepped back and let her walk from the room.

Hillary started to follow and then looked back at Anton and Inez.

"I don't understand the two of you," she said. "Half the women in this country under the age of thirty would gladly change places with Constance, and you act as if she's either sold her soul to the devil or she's getting ready to commit suicide. I just can't understand why."

Inez sighed deeply as she faced Hillary. "There is a reason."

"Mom. No."

Inez shook her head. "You know, Anton, I

think maybe it's time we said it." She shared a long, probing look with her son before again turning to Hillary. "Constance is not my daughter."

Hillary looked at the woman in confusion and then the impact of her words struck her.

"Oh, Inez, Constance told me she was adopted, but surely that...surely after all these years... She *is* your child whether she was born to you or not. And even if...what difference does that make anyway?"

Inez threw back her head and took a deep breath. "None, in the way you're thinking, and yet every difference in the world."

Inez reached for Anton's hand. "Constance is my granddaughter."

Hillary's startled glance flew to Anton's face. *Her granddaughter?* Unbidden, she remembered Constance's words, *He was more father to me than he was brother.* Oh, Lord! The suspicion had barely formed when she realized Inez was still speaking, softly, so softly she had to strain to hear.

"She's Florence's child."

Chapter Twelve

At Inez's insistence, the three of them moved to Anton's study. Hillary went silently, stunned by Inez's revelation, and even more stunned by how readily she had been willing to accept suspicion of Anton.

Florence's child. Her thoughts returned to those words. Constance was the daughter of that beautiful girl in the picture in the hallway. That explained the uncanny resemblance the three of them bore to one another. That explained the similarity in mannerisms and reactions Hillary had seen in Constance and Anton. But it left so much more open to question.

Shaded lamps cast soft pools of light in Anton's study, leaving the rest of the room in shadows. Hillary seated herself uneasily on one end of the ivory-colored sofa. Inez, equally ill at ease, sat on the other end of the sofa.

Anton looked from Hillary to his mother and then turned to leave the room.

"No," Inez said softly. "Please stay."

"I don't think Hillary needs to hear this," he said. "I know I don't."

"But I need to say it."

He stared at his mother for long moments, as though willing her to silence, before walking to his desk and leaning against it.

He was poised for flight, Hillary thought as she watched him. How strange it was to see him not totally in control of a situation.

"We aren't blind to Constance's needs, Hillary," Inez said. "And we aren't unfeeling. We aren't prejudiced without reason."

Inez sat primly on the edge of the sofa, with her feet flat on the floor and her hands clasped tightly in her lap.

"We're afraid."

Hillary heard the quiver in the woman's voice and the softly muttered expletive from Anton. She remained silent, not knowing what to say.

"There's quite an age difference in my children," Inez continued hesitantly. "After Ben and Timothy, I...I lost two babies before Florence was born. She was special to me because of that, because I thought I'd never have any more children, and because she was a much-needed softness in my life."

Inez swallowed and twisted her hands together. "Three years later, Anton was an added blessing. Things were so different then from the way they are now. Then it seemed as though life was nothing but never-ending work, trying to eke out a living, trying to hold this place together.

"I tried to protect my two younger children from that as much as I could, because I hadn't been able to protect the two older ones. But even with that, they both had responsibilities far greater than a child should have to bear.

"One of Florence's was caring for Anton, because I was needed in the fields. They developed a closeness, a bond that excluded their father. At times I thought, then, that it even excluded me."

She looked up at her son. "I know better now.

"Florence didn't look delicate. None of us ever *looked* delicate. But she was a dreamer, a romantic. And much too gentle for the life she was born into. I still have some of her early poetry."

Inez twisted on the sofa to face Hillary. "Which really doesn't explain anything," she said, "except…"

Inez swallowed again, and continued, "Except…when Florence was seventeen, a group of young men came to the winery. We didn't have organized tours then, but we did have a retail outlet, of sorts. They were musicians. Their band was playing in a club in Fort Smith and, bored with what the town had to offer, they had taken the suggestion of the owner of the club and had decided to tour the countryside.

"Florence was fascinated by them, and by the excitement and glamour she thought they had in their lives. One of them, apparently, was fascinated by her. He came back several times in the next week. He was too old for her, too knowledgeable, too experienced. I saw it and didn't know what to do except pray that he'd move on before any lasting damage was done.

"He flattered her, he flirted with her, he admired her poetry. By the time her father realized what was happening, Florence had convinced herself she was in love with the young man.

"She made a date with him to go into Fort Smith to watch him perform. When her father found out, he refused to let her go. There was a horrible scene between them that night that I'll never forget. He locked her in her room. She... she left by an upstairs window.

"A month later, we got a letter from her. I recognized her handwriting, but all I had a chance to see on the envelope was part of the return address. She was somewhere in Texas. Her father had the letter. He wouldn't let me have it. 'She's made her choice,' he said. 'We have nothing to say to her. This one's going back, too.' I couldn't believe that he wouldn't even let me open it, that there had been others that he hadn't told me about.

"Anton... Anton tried to take the letter from him, but at fourteen he was no match for his father's strength."

Inez closed her eyes for a moment, and when she opened them, her erect posture, if anything, became more disciplined.

"It was a year before we heard anything else. If I hadn't answered the telephone, we might still not know. The call was from a hospital in Wyoming. Florence was dead. Her baby, Constance, was not expected to live.

"I left immediately, not even asking permission. Anton went with me. We saw the room where my beautiful daughter had spent the last months of her life, alone, in poverty. Where the man she had loved, the man for whom she had given up her family, had abandoned her. We read the poetry she wrote during that time, poetry filled with the quiet desperation she couldn't share with anyone."

Silent tears streamed down Inez's face. "Do you know how cold it is in Wyoming in the winter? We buried Florence there, in the cold, and all I have left of her is her poetry, and her daughter.

"When Constance was strong enough to travel, we brought her home. I defied my husband for the first time in our married life. I refused to give up the baby. But I did compromise with him. He insisted we go through legal adoption, to change the names on the birth certificate, so the world wouldn't know his shame."

"Inez..." Hillary reached for the woman but let her hand drop ineffectually to the sofa cushion.

"I never forgave him, Hillary. I never forgot. And I never forgave myself, either, because if I had been stronger, that wouldn't have happened. But I am stronger now. I can't watch it happen to Constance, too."

Hillary felt tears on her own cheeks. She longed

to reach out and comfort Inez, to hold her to herself. "It isn't the same," she said softly. "Can't
you see that?"

"I want to believe that, Hillary," Inez said.
"But I can't. I . . . just . . . can't."

Inez rose unsteadily to her feet. In an instant,
Anton was beside her. Hillary watched Inez lean
against him, crying silently, drawing strength from
him before she pulled away from him and walked
proudly from the room.

Anton remained motionless until his mother
pulled the door shut behind her. Then he shifted
slightly to look down at Hillary.

"Now you know all the secrets," he said.
"What are you going to do?"

"Do?" she asked numbly, still caught in Florence's tragedy. Although his face was masked in
shadow, she read wariness and distrust in his
voice.

She shook her head and rested her face in her
hands.

Do? What on earth did he think she would do
with Inez's trust? Run from neighbor to neighbor
telling the story? Post a notice in the church? Sell
it to a tabloid?

"You really don't think much of me as a person, do you?" she asked, still cradling her face in
her hands.

Anton's silence was the answer she had dreaded, and expected, and the end to all her hopes of
ever gaining his trust or his love. She drew herself
erect and stood facing him. Only then did she see

his face. He was hurting. She longed to hold him, to let him draw strength from her, to comfort him. But she was hurting, too, so much that she couldn't risk opening herself to any more.

"At fourteen, you couldn't have changed a thing," she said, sensing that he, too, carried guilt for what had happened. "Now you can. Tell her, Anton."

Hillary hesitated, stopped by the fleeting thought of how encouraging this revelation was somehow disloyal to Tippy, but she pushed that thought away. She wasn't taking—couldn't take—sides in something as important as this.

"Tell Constance why you feel the way you do. She needs to understand. It's tearing her apart, Anton."

"No."

He had carefully blanked all expression from his eyes and from his voice.

"Not now."

"But why? Do you know how much she wants to belong to this family? *Really* belong?"

"She should have been told," he said, interrupting her, "long ago. But that wasn't my decision to make, then or now."

"Then talk to Inez. Ask her. *Convince* her. Constance needs to know."

"I can't put her through that again!"

"You can't?" Hillary wanted to shake him. "You can't put her through the pain of talking about it, so you're willing to let her relive the reality?"

Suspicion glittered in the midnight depths of his eyes. Beneath the softness of his mustache, his mouth tightened.

"Oh, not her death," Hillary said. "That's not going to happen. She isn't Florence, and Tippy isn't that unfeeling bastard. But losing her. Can't you see? You're forcing her to choose, Anton. *Forcing* her. And you're driving her away just as surely as your father kept Florence away! Tell her, Anton," she pleaded. "Or let me."

"Hillary, you were told in confidence." She heard an unspoken threat in his voice. "You can't tell her."

She was exhausted from hurling herself against the wall of his stubbornness and aching from her own pain.

"Oh, I see," she said, not trying to hide the bitterness that crept into her voice. "There's no way out of this pit you've assigned me to, is there?" She felt her mouth twisting in derision. "Damned if I do? And damned if I don't?"

"What are you talking about?"

"You know very well what I'm talking about!" Her anger was rising, pushing out the pain. "If I betray your confidence, I'll just prove to you again how devious I am. Tell me, Anton, how do you measure it? Will it be more reprehensible, or less, than not betraying Constance's confidence?"

"It isn't the same," she heard him say, realizing that he was patronizing her, attempting to placate her.

"And why not?" Oh, Lord, it felt so good, at

last, not to have to be defensive. "Because for once you can't lay the blame for something at my feet? Because for once there's no way I can be responsible for your pain? I'm sorry, really sorry, that I can't oblige you by taking that blame, too."

She choked back a harsh laugh. "Excuse me, but I've been laboring under a mistaken impression of my own importance for the last several days. You see, I accepted that I was to blame... for all of it."

"Hillary..." He reached for her.

"No!" She shrugged away from him. "I've said I'm sorry, forgive me and let me explain, until I almost forgot there were any other words. And why? Because you let me. You didn't have to tell me the whole story, maybe not any of it. A simple 'It's not your fault' would have been sufficient. But no, you let me go on thinking, you fostered those thoughts, you *accused* me with every word, every action. And why was that? Because you wanted me to hurt as much as you had? Well, you got your wish."

Hillary felt the pressure of tears behind her eyes. She couldn't cry, not now. She couldn't give him that victory, too.

"But you didn't have to wish for it, Anton. The pain you wanted me to feel is a replay of what I felt when I left the first time. You should be pleased."

Not looking away from him, carefully she began walking toward the door. One step at a time. That was all she had to take, just one step at a time, and she would reach the safety of the door-

way. Then she could break eye contact with him.
Then she could turn. And then—oh, God, could
she hold out that long?—then she could give in to
the tears building within her.

She reached the door and groped for the knob.
He had not moved. Nothing about his face revealed his thoughts. She forced herself to look
away from his eyes. His stance—yes, she realized,
he had masked his feelings from her, but his
stance, coiled and waiting, betrayed him.

Betrayed him how? She could no more read the
cause of his tension than she could read his mind.
He was a willful, stubborn, proud man, locked in
a shell of his own making. Alone, as he had been
for years. Why hadn't she seen that before? As he
would always be, unless . . .

"Anton?" She couldn't keep the softness from
her voice. "Let her go." Would he even understand the difference? "Don't drive her away."

His mask slipped, only a little, but she saw the
pain once again in his eyes before he turned his
back to her and walked to the window.

Hillary stared at the unyielding breadth of his
shoulders. For a moment she considered throwing her own pride away and going to him. She
sagged against the door. No, she couldn't do that;
that would solve nothing.

She slipped quietly from the room, leaving him
alone, looking out into the night.

STILL GROGGY FROM TOO LITTLE SLEEP, Hillary tried
to decide what had awakened her. Had she heard a

door slam? Or had that been only another part of one of the fragmented dreams that had haunted her through the early-morning hours? A dream, she decided as she rearranged her pillow and closed her eyes against the bright morning light.

It was late. She sensed that. She ought to get up. She knew that for a fact. *Why?* she argued with herself. To face more of what she had faced the last week and a half? To put on her cheerful "look at what a nice person I am" smile? Not today, thank you. Maybe not ever again.

It hadn't done any good. The only thing she had managed to do in the entire week and a half she'd been there was to exhaust herself, physically and emotionally, and now—damn it—she couldn't even go back to sleep.

She tossed the sheet away from her, swung her legs around and sat limply on the side of the bed.

And she couldn't leave. If the night before had convinced her that there was no life for her here, it had also finally convinced her that Connie really did need her to stay.

Hillary heard another loud, indefinable noise from somewhere within the house. Curiosity was what finally got her on her feet. Curiosity in the thought that maybe it hadn't been a dream that had awakened her after all. Curiosity that was soon quenched when the recorded sounds of Tippy's band and Tippy's voice reverberated through the house, played at what must approach maximum volume and definitely at maximum bass.

Constance. What had happened now?

Hillary felt a twinge of remorse for not having gone to the young woman the night before, but after all that had happened she hadn't been able to. She just hadn't been able to.

Now she had no choice and no excuse.

Was Constance trying to alienate her family completely? If so, this adolescent stunt would certainly help.

Hillary paused only long enough to belt a robe around her and run a brush through her hair as she grimaced at her wan reflection in the mirror before running upstairs and knocking on Constance's door. And knocking. And finally balling her hand into a fist and pounding on the door, competing with the noise, because at that volume it couldn't be called music coming from inside the room.

Constance finally threw open the door. When she saw Hillary, her belligerent scowl turned to a look of pure chagrin.

"Oh," she said. At least that's what Hillary thought she said, because hearing words was impossible.

Hillary stepped around Constance and twisted the volume control on the stereo down to a level that would permit conversation.

"If you're not worried about my hearing or yours," she said evenly, "you ought at least to be concerned about abusing your speakers."

Hillary massaged her forehead with the fingers of one hand. If everything else wasn't already enough, now she felt the beginnings of what promised to be a monumental headache. "All right," she said. "Do you want to talk?"

Constance flounced onto the bed and tucked her knees under her chin. Her belligerence was back.

"Constance..." The open suitcase had been moved from the bed to the one chair. If anything, its contents looked even more tumbled than they had been the night before. Hillary considered moving the suitcase to the floor but changed her mind when she realized that Constance's attitude was only thinly masking hurt. She smoothed a place on the unmade bed next to Constance and sat beside her.

"Are you trying to make things worse than they already are?" Hillary asked carefully.

Constance's chin quivered, but she held on to her rigid pose. "Why would I want to do that?"

"I don't know," Hillary said. She glanced at the two dormer windows that had been flung open. "Is it quiet at the winery this morning?"

"Why?" Constance asked sharply.

"Oh..." Hillary shook her head. "Constance, I don't think, even as loud as it was, your impromptu concert was heard by anyone but the two of us, but if it had been...why are you deliberately trying to provoke your brother and to hurt your mother?"

"Hillary, can we leave, you and I, today? Now?"

Leave? Oh, how Hillary wanted to do just that—escape from the whole unbearable situation, forget it had ever happened. But too much was at stake.

"Running away doesn't solve anything," she said, smiling grimly. "I tried it once, remember?"

"What was it like?" Constance asked. "I mean, how did you feel when..."

"When I made my escape?"

Constance's aggressive attitude had slackened. She looked unsure of herself and, Hillary thought, embarrassed by her question but in need of an answer. "Yes."

"Scared," Hillary said honestly. "At first. I didn't plan it, you know. It just happened. And then—when I realized that Jay wasn't going to be able to stop me—free." Hillary remembered the intoxication of that fleeting feeling. "Absolutely free for the first time in years, maybe ever. But that didn't last long. Because by cutting myself off from what had hurt me, I also cut myself off from those who loved me, and I had to face how alone I really was."

"And then you met Anton," Constance prompted with uncharacteristic shyness.

"Yes." Hillary didn't want to be reminded, but it was too late, too late for too many things. "And lost him."

"Are you sure, Hillary? Absolutely sure?"

After the scene in Anton's study the night before, Hillary had no doubts. "I'm sure."

"How..." Constance asked hesitantly, "How did you meet him?"

What good would it do to dredge up the old

memories, Hillary wondered. But Constance's belligerence was finally gone, and Hillary found a strange sort of solace in being able to talk about those long-suppressed memories.

"I was at the church. I didn't mean to come there. I didn't even know this place existed. I stumbled on to St. Mary's by accident, and...it seemed to symbolize all the things I didn't have in my life—family and permanence and caring and...love. You know how, when things are almost too much to bear, some little thing, something so minor as to be almost inconsequential when things are going well can...can...My little thing was not being able to play the organ in the church. I had never wanted anything so much, at that particular moment, as to fill that church, to surround myself, to lose myself with the power of that organ. I broke. I ran out of the church. But I had already run away. There wasn't any place else to run. Anton found me crying in the cemetery."

Constance reached for Hillary's hand. "I'm sorry. I didn't mean to ruin things for you."

"Connie, Connie," Hillary said, forcing her words past the constriction in her throat. "It was ruined before it began."

"I can do one thing for you," Constance offered hesitantly. "It doesn't seem like much now, but if you want...if you still want to play the organ, I can arrange for you to."

"And pump it for me?" Hillary asked. "Thanks, Constance, but I..."

"It's been electrified. You won't need anyone

to pump it. And I don't think you want anyone there to intrude, do you?''

Hillary looked up at her through a quick mist of tears. ''No,'' she said.

''Go get dressed,'' Constance urged, ''and have some breakfast. I'll call the rectory. The organ loft will be unlocked when you get there.''

HILLARY KNELT FOR A LONG TIME at the back pew. The church was as she remembered, unchanged and ageless. Strong sunlight through the stained-glass windows cast patterns of rose and gold and blue across the dark pews and light walls. Behind the altar, the high, blue dome with its delicate paintings promised coolness and peace.

She had found the front doors propped open when she arrived, and those portions of the windows that could be opened were open, but already Hillary's hair clung damply to her neck and trickles of moisture crept down her back.

Had it been this warm when she visited before? It was funny, she'd thought she'd never forget anything about that day, but here was one fact she couldn't remember. Maybe with time the others would fade, too. The organ loft would be a furnace, with the heat trapped between it and the high ceiling of the building. She roused herself from her reverie and made her way up the narrow stairs. The grate was unlocked, and the organ uncovered, switched on and waiting.

She made a mental note of the position of the stops before she reset them. Bach, she had wanted four years ago, and Bach it would be to-day.

She ran her fingers over the opening notes and waited while the message was sent from the keyboard to the bellows, until the music burst forth from the pipes behind her.

"Good-bye," she whispered. But her words and her choked sob were obliterated by the music, the glorious, purging, healing music that poured from her and through her.

Bach, yes, she played Bach, and selections from Handel, from Wagner, from Mahler, until her skin glistened with moisture. How fitting, she thought, one of the few clear thoughts she allowed herself, every pore of her body was crying. She played everything she could remember that echoed the turmoil she held in her soul until she had no more strength. Then she drifted into the gentle music of "Greensleeves" and then into silence.

"I go into the vineyards." Anton spoke guardedly. His voice was low and hoarse.

Hillary closed her eyes, knowing it was impossible to hide her vulnerability from him now.

"Among the vines that I planted, that I nurtured. It's the only place that I've ever been able to lose myself," he said. "Or to find myself. But lately, even that hasn't brought me much peace."

Trying to calm her racing heart, she began resetting the organ stops. "How did you find me?"

"Constance."

"Have you been here long?"

"Yes."

She turned to him, beyond caring what her appearance said about her weakened defenses. "Why?"

"Hillary," he said raggedly. He drew a deep breath. She saw in him an answering vulnerability that he made no attempt to hide. "I thought you were gone. Until I found Constance, I thought both of you were gone."

"I see," she said. She slumped desolately on the bench. "You thought I had taken your sister and run away with her?"

"No."

She looked up at him in surprise.

"I thought I had done what you accused me of last night. I thought I had driven her away. I thought I had driven you away. Have I, Hillary?"

Hillary looked out over the church, not willing and not able to meet the probing questions in his eyes.

"Do you think that I would sell Constance to Bill Roeffler for a few miserable acres of land?"

"No," she admitted. "For a while, last night, it seemed possible. But no, Anton. You could never do that."

"She won't let me explain. She's closed herself off from me. She refuses to listen to me. She said some cutting, painful things to me, Hillary."

"That's to be expected. She's hurting."

"And you, Hillary. Are you hurting?"

Oh, God! She drew in a sharp breath and refused to let herself crumple before him.

"Because what Constance said to me reminded me mercilessly of the things I've said to you."

"Don't," she whispered. "Please, don't."

He took a step closer to her, and another. She drew herself upright, willing him not to touch her.

"We have to talk," he said. "After all we've said to each other, we finally have to talk. But not here, and not now. Tonight?" he said. "Away from the house. Away from any possible interruption. Will you give me that much more? Can you?"

She forced herself to meet his eyes, but she wouldn't, couldn't, let herself feel any hope at his words. Numbly, she nodded.

A hesitant smile softened the harsh lines of his face. "Tonight," he repeated, but Hillary couldn't tell if that softly spoken word carried a threat or a promise.

Chapter Thirteen

A strangely subdued Constance sat cross-legged on the bed while Hillary riffled through the few clothes in her closet.

"I didn't know he meant dinner," Hillary muttered.

"What did you think he had in mind?" Constance asked. "A quiet walk in the moonlight when it's still ninety-five degrees outside. Or maybe you could go down to the winery and weigh in grapes and stop periodically to check on the fermentation of the Niagara." She softened her words with a smile.

"Hillary, it's only dinner."

She unwound herself from the bed and pushed past Hillary, reaching into the closet. "Here, wear this," she said, handing Hillary the one dress she had brought with her, a long-sleeved green silk with a soft cowl collar and gently gathered skirt.

"He's probably going to take you to Wiederkehr's, unless he wants to drive half the night, and if he does, you'll need those sleeves."

"Constance, are you sure you'll be all right? You've acted so strangely today. First this morning, and you've been quiet all afternoon."

"I'm fine," Constance said. "I've just had a lot to think about." She chuckled mirthlessly. "You ought to know that. Besides, I've already eaten a sandwich, and with Mom at a special meeting of the Altar Guild and you and Anton out of the house, finally I'm going to be able to get to work on my song."

"But I . . ."

"You're scared to death," Constance said.

"No, I . . ." Oh, what was the use in denying it? "Yes, I am."

"It's time I returned something to you." Constance reached into the pocket of her shorts and drew out a gold necklace.

"Ludwig," Hillary said as she looked at the frenzied, wild-haired caricature. "I'd forgotten you had him."

"Your talisman? I've kept him close," she admitted. "But now you need him more than I do."

"No." Hillary shook her head. "This evening is going to be hard enough without openly reminding Anton of that part of my life."

"Don't be ridiculous. Weren't you the one who told me that you couldn't go on stage or give an interview without having the necklace with you?"

"That was different, Constance."

"Maybe not. You can wear it underneath your collar, or carry it with you if that's too much, but I think you need it tonight."

Hillary clenched the necklace in her hand. It was irrational, she knew it, but true.

"Do you know what he wants to talk about?"

Hillary had a fairly good idea, but obviously Constance hadn't been told of any of the conversation of the previous night.

"You, I'm sure," she said and watched the warmth die in Constance's gray eyes. "Other than that . . . other than that, I have not let myself think about what will be said."

"It will be all right," Constance told her, giving her a quick hug that carried an intensity of emotion far greater than her words. "Now, you finish getting dressed. I'm going to try to find the staff paper I hid somewhere in this house last summer."

ANTON HAD DRESSED CASUALLY in well-tailored dark slacks and a knit shirt that showed off the breadth of his shoulders and sleekly corded muscles of his arms. She met him in his study. Awkwardly silent, they walked to his car.

Constance had guessed correctly. He took her to Wiederkehr's, only a short distance from his own winery. The Weinkeller restaurant was located in the original cellars of the Wiederkehr winery. And Constance was also right that Hillary would need the long sleeves of her dress in the dim coolness of the room.

With only a little gentle teasing from the hostess about spying on the competition, she and Anton were seated in a quiet corner of the restaurant at a table made from an old wine cask. The waitress, costumed to complement the Swiss Chalet theme, lighted a new candle and positioned it in the multicolored wax-covered wine bottle in the center of the table. She opened the menus and left them to make their choices.

Hillary glanced around the room. She could see only subtle changes from the way it had looked four years ago, the last time she had been there with Anton. And that night—the print on her menu swam before her eyes—that night she had been dreading a talk with him almost as much as she dreaded this one.

"Do you want the quiche?" Anton asked. "Or do you want to try something different?"

"The quiche," she said, venturing a small smile toward him, grateful for the distraction of ordering. "I still can't believe anything is that good."

She let him order the meal and wine from the Wiederkehr list—quiche for her, accompanied by the Johannesberg Riesling he recommended, steak with wine sauce for him, and Pinot Noir. For the next half hour, or longer—the time seemed interminable to Hillary—they were engrossed by the service of the meal, by the mechanics of eating.

The food was excellent. Hillary knew that. Was it too much to hope that one day she would be able really to enjoy a meal in this restaurant?

When the dishes had been cleared and coffee poured, Anton leaned back against the wall behind him and slanted a glance at Hillary.

It's time, she thought, *and he's as tense as I am.*

"Will you tell me..." He took a deep breath, and she watched his hand clench around his coffee cup. "I know you've told me parts of it before. I know I have no right to ask it of you now. But will you tell me about... Jay, and Tippy, and me?"

Hillary's own knuckles were white as she held her cup in both hands. Yes, she had told him, at least parts of it, and she had wondered as she did so how much he really heard. She had wanted to scream at him, to make him listen to her, and now he was asking.

So she told him. She told him how Elaine, even though she was divorced from her father, had left Tippy with her that one summer, not in her care but in her company, while Elaine went to Europe. How she had been doing graduate work. How she had staged a summer production of *Bye-Bye Birdie*. How she had cast Tippy in the starring role. How Jay had happened to be in the audience. How Elaine had refused to sign a contract for the underaged boy. How Jay had then courted her, and married her, only to gain Elaine's confidence and Tippy's contract.

"I had been brought up to believe that marriage was forever," she told Anton, "that the husband was the head of the family. And I so wanted to be a part of a family. But Jay didn't want a wife. He didn't want a family. He didn't, God forbid, want children. He wanted money and status and recognition. And Tippy brought him all three. But in getting that he had also saddled himself with a wife.

"I can tell you to the day when he decided that he could exploit what talent I had. I argued with him. I already knew that I wasn't a performer and, if I had been, not the commercially acceptable kind he wanted me to be. But eventually, I gave in. After all, what's a little pride when your marriage is at stake?

"When Tippy and I first heard the rumors about ourselves, we laughed. We knew they weren't true. There didn't even seem to be any reason to dispute them. We weren't technically related by then. Elaine and my father had been divorced for years. I don't know how the tabloids missed out on that piece of information—unless, of course, Jay had decided they didn't need to know that. And it was Jay who started the rumors; after all, scandal sells papers. It was just so much free publicity to him. We learned that, much too late. By the time we decided that we needed to do something about the stories, it was much too late for that, too. The damage had already been done.

"I put up with it as long as I could, until one night..."

Her voice caught. Not even now could she talk about that night. "Until one night, Jay went too far. I didn't think about it; I was beyond thinking at that point. I just ran."

Only then did she look away from the depths of

her coffee. Anton was still holding his cup, not drinking from it, perhaps not even aware of it, just clutching it.

"It was a fantasy," she said. "I put myself through torture. My reputation was ruined. I prostituted my talent. I had twisted myself inside out for two years—for a fantasy."

He had asked about Jay and Tippy, and Hillary had recited those facts emotionlessly. He had also asked about himself. That part would be harder, she knew. She had tried so many times to convince him. *Once more,* she told herself. *Once more.* If she could reach him, it would be worth baring her emotions, again.

"And then I found you. You were my reality, Anton. You offered me everything I had ever wanted, and I was terrified of losing you. That's why I couldn't tell you who I was. And that's why, when I went back, I wouldn't take your calls. That's why I didn't tell anyone about you. You don't take something perfect and drag it through the mud I had to go through. You just don't."

Anton put his coffee cup on the table, splashing the now cold liquid into the saucer. "Let's go," he said abruptly.

Let's go? She had just stripped herself of her last vestige of pride, and all he could say was "Let's go"? She fumbled blindly for her purse. "All right."

Anton had parked in the drive beyond the restaurant. There were few cars there. Most patrons parked in the large lot by the gift shop. Numbly,

Hillary walked to the car and waited for him to unlock the door.

She felt his hands on her shoulders. He turned her to face him.

"I loved you, Hillary."

She closed her eyes. Now she knew why executioners used blindfolds. Darkness was infinitely preferable to watching your own destruction.

"I have never exposed myself the way I did, loving you, with anyone else. When you left, I had to convince myself I hated you—or go crazy. And after all, who was I? A winemaker. And not a very profitable one at the time. I had worked all my life and I was just at the point where I could say, maybe, one day, I'd be able to see results from that work. You had Tippy Grey and Jay Weston and half the press in the country clamoring at your door. I had to believe that our time had been only a game for you. I had to believe that you had used me. I had to be able to get angry, to stay angry. Can you understand that?"

She opened her eyes, daring to look up at him, daring to hope.

Shadows. They were always in shadows. Why could she never see his face?

"Oh, Anton..."

He bent to her. His lips took hers in a questioning kiss. He pulled away and returned for another. And another. She caught his face in her hands to hold him to her, answering the question she sensed with her lips, her body.

His arms crushed her to him. There was no

question in this kiss. It devastated her with its power. She quivered in his arms, molded against him and yet not close enough. She felt his hands moving over her, claiming her, and she willingly relinquished possession to him.

He pulled away from her, breathing raggedly. He folded her against his chest, and she felt the erratic beat of his heart.

"Let's go home," he said unevenly.

Home. Home in Anton's arms. It was the only place she ever wanted to be. Wanting him was a painful ache that threatened to consume her.

"It's early," she murmured. "Constance is . . ."

His arms tightened around her. "Oh, damn," she heard him whisper.

Across the drive, the door to the club opened. She heard laughter floating on the night air and strains of music from inside the building. A female vocalist was singing "Crazy Blue Eyes." She found herself smiling in spite of the frustrated desire still twisting through her. One day she would sing that song for Anton the way she had written it. One day she would tell him how she had written it for him. One day he would be ready to hear that.

For now she would give what he would let her, and take what he was willing to give. At last he was reaching out to her, emotionally as well as physically. And the confidences he had shared seemed monumental in light of her new knowledge of how private and guarded his life had been.

There was hope. Held in the protection of his

arms, Hillary allowed herself to believe that there was hope—for herself, for the love she and Anton had once shared, even for Constance. Surely now, now that he had taken this step, he wouldn't again lock himself in rigid prejudice.

Her cheek rested over his heart, his chin on her head, as he held her. She felt his hands moving restlessly over her. He shifted slightly, bringing them closer together and bent his head to her. "I want to love you," he whispered.

Hillary didn't know how he meant the word "love"—love as used to describe the physical act, or love as used to describe the torrent of emotions she felt for him. She doubted that he could sort through his feelings and explain what he really meant. It didn't matter. At least not at that moment. Now it was enough that he was turning to her, not away. She slid her hands up the solid strength of his back and turned her face to his.

She saw passion in his eyes, but she also saw an openness that she had not seen in years. The doubts were gone. The wariness was gone.

She closed her eyes as he claimed her mouth—closed her eyes and opened her heart, welcoming him to her.

Headlights separated them, headlights bearing down on them. Tires slid on loose gravel, sending it scattering in sharp little showers.

"What idiot...?" Anton pushed her behind him as he turned toward the pickup truck now stopped only a few feet from them.

The door of the truck opened and then slammed

shut before she saw the driver. Bill stood in the drive, breathing heavily. A trickle of blood oozed from a swelling bruise on his lip.

"I hoped I'd find you here."

"What's wrong?" Anton asked tersely.

"Was it worth it, cousin?" Bill shot her a glance full of anger and derision. "Constance is gone."

"Gone?" Hillary and Anton spoke as one.

"Gone. As in 'split.' Left. Cleared out. And isn't it a coincidence that her boyfriend knew exactly when you and Inez would both be out of the house?"

"Tippy . . . ?" Hillary began.

"Come off it, Hillary," Bill said. "You can drop the act now."

"Where is my mother?" Anton asked. "Does she know?"

Bill stared insolently at Anton. "She's still at the church. I came looking for you first because I wasn't sure where I'd find you or what you'd be doing."

Anton fished his keys from his pocket and unlocked the car.

"What do you want me to do?" Bill asked.

Anton's gaze flicked over him, lingering on the split lip. "Nothing," he said. "I don't want you to do anything. Or say anything. Do you understand me?"

Anton took Hillary by the arm and pulled her toward the car. "Get in."

Those were the only words he spoke. He drove to the church, taking the curves and turns competently but with a determination and speed that chilled Hillary.

She waited in the car while he went into the parish hall. A few minutes later, she watched as he and Inez walked from the hall. Inez was laughing about something. Anton put his hands on her shoulders and stopped her, telling her before they returned to the car. Hillary could hear only the murmur of their voices—Anton's deep and intense, Inez's shocked and disbelieving. She saw Inez put a hand to her mouth and sway against Anton, but by the time they reached the car, Inez had herself as tightly under control as Anton.

Anton spoke to her only once during the silent vigil. He turned to her and asked her in a voice devoid of emotion, "What do you know about this?"

She had been foolish enough to think he wouldn't again lock himself away from her. How wrong she had been.

She met his eyes, refusing to look away. "Nothing."

Sometime during the night, Hillary went upstairs. No one stopped her. No one followed. It took only a few minutes to separate her things from those of Carla's that Inez had lent her, only a few minutes to pack her small suitcase, only a few minutes to remove every trace of herself from the room.

She set her case on the floor by the door and looked back at the room where she had known ecstasy and despair.

She was furious with both Constance and Tippy. She had expected more maturity, and more consideration for the persons who loved them, than either had shown in this last rash act. But she wouldn't voice that anger. She wouldn't voice anything in this silent, lonely house. She would wait until a decent hour or until the two young people telephoned, whichever came first, and then she would escape from the unspoken, unfounded accusations she knew were directed at her.

And she wouldn't come back to this room. The memories here were too poignant. She picked up her suitcase and carried it downstairs. Then, only because there was nothing else she could do, she joined Anton and Inez in Anton's study, and waited.

THE TELEPHONE CALL CAME at nine o'clock in the morning. Anton snatched up the receiver on the first ring.

"It's for you." He held the receiver out to Hillary but didn't step away when she took it.

"Hillary Michaels?" It was a long-distance operator's impersonal voice.

"Yes."

"Hillary?" Tippy's slightly gravelly voice, the voice that sent millions of women into erotic fantasy, grated across her tightly strung nerves.

"Where are you?" she asked in a tone demanding an immediate answer.

"Vegas. We flew out here last night. We're married, Hillary. There's nothing they can do about it now." His voice had taken on an abrasive, aggressive quality, but it softened with the next words. "Are you all right?"

No, she was not all right. She might never be all right again. "Why, Tippy? Why did you sneak in like this? Why couldn't the two of you have waited? It was only a few more days. Do either of you have any concept..."

"I didn't sneak, Hillary," he said, interrupting her. "I told you I was coming."

"Told me...? Oh, my God. But you... But I..."

"You weren't very encouraging, and I thought I might wait after all, but Connie has been so evasive the last few days, I had to find out for myself what was going on. It's a damned good thing I did, too." Hillary heard the growing anger in his voice. "When I got there, that 'good old boy' they've been trying to push her into marrying had Connie trapped in a corner. She was almost in hysterics," he said. "We had to leave. We can sort it out with her family later. After they have accepted the fact that they can't do anything about the marriage. After they have accepted the fact that *I'm* taking care of Connie now and I'm not going to let them do anything else to hurt her."

"Oh, Tippy," Hillary moaned. "It's not that way."

"Forget about them," he said. "It's you I'm worried about. I hate having left you there in that position, but I had to get Connie away. Now answer me, are you all right?"

She considered lying to him—for only a second.

His life had pushed him into an appearance of maturity beyond his years, but as he spoke she realized that was all it was—an appearance. The time had long passed for her to stop protecting him.

"No, Tippy, I'm not all right. Nothing about this situation is all right. And it won't be until the four of you—you, Constance, Anton and Inez—stop hurling accusations and hiding fears about each other."

"Hillary..."

"Don't Hillary me in that tone of voice, Tippy Grey!" She remembered her audience then, two persons who had to be avidly interested in every word, and she remembered that her anger and frustration were deeply entwined with so many things that it wasn't fair to let Tippy bear the full force of it. She slumped against the desk, trying not to feel the close scrutiny that Anton subjected her to. "Never mind, Tippy. We'll talk later."

"You're sure? Hillary, I didn't mean to—"

"I know, Tippy," she said, sighing. "And I understand."

"Connie wants to talk to you."

Hillary waited—no answer was necessary—while Tippy handed the phone to Constance.

"Hillary?" Constance sounded so much like a child waiting for her punishment that Hillary couldn't direct any anger at her.

"Yes, Constance?"

"Do you remember what you said, that you didn't really plan to run away, you just did it?"

Oh, yes, she remembered. All too clearly.

"Well..." Constance paused before continuing in a rush, "Well, that's not exactly what happened. I mean, I knew Tippy was coming, and after what happened Tuesday night, when Bill said what he did, I really did want to run away. That's why I acted the way I did yesterday. I wanted Anton to get mad, really mad, you know, so I could storm out of there and it would all be his fault. But he wouldn't do it ... and ... after I talked to you, I knew I couldn't leave you there that way. I was going to stay, Hillary. Really I was. Until Bill ... and then I just couldn't help it, I had to leave. Say you understand, Hillary. Please?"

"Constance..." Hillary took a deep breath and gathered her thoughts. "I understand," she said, "but I'm not the one you need to tell. Anton and Inez are both here. You need to talk to them."

"Hillary! Couldn't you..."

"No."

Hillary waited through the long silence until Constance whispered, "Mom."

She held out the receiver. Anton reached for it. Hillary stopped him with a quick shake of her head. "Inez."

Hillary heard the soft murmur of Inez's conversation, but it was Anton she watched. The sleepless night had taken its toll. He needed a shave, she thought irrelevantly. He needed sleep. Deep grooves etched their way on each side of his mouth, hidden only partially by his mustache. His eyes, his beautiful blue eyes, which had been the first thing she noticed about him, were now lightly veined and rimmed with a trace of red. But he held himself in tight control, control that slipped only when Inez hung up the telephone without handing it to him and then was immediately clamped back into place.

Inez looked at Anton without speaking.

The silence settled over them until it filled the room.

It was time for Hillary to leave, but, perversely, the silence held her prisoner. She couldn't leave unless she broke it.

"They're married." She spoke to Anton. "I was as against it as you when Tippy first told me their plans," she said, "but for different reasons. Maybe they are too young. Last night would certainly indicate that. But they *are* married. And they are going to have a child. And whether you believe it or not, they do love each other.

"I'm sorry that they did things the way they did, but I can't be sorry that they found each other."

Anton remained as motionless as the rock from which his cellars were dug.

Hillary's face twisted in a bitter smile. "And I didn't have anything to do with it, but I don't suppose you can ever believe that, can you?"

He moved then, slowly, as though awakening from a deep sleep. He ran his hand impatiently through his hair. "Hillary, I don't know what to believe anymore."

She caught a fleeting glimpse of vulnerability in his eyes. Oh, no, she thought. Not again. Not ever again. "Don't bother," she said. She had torn herself apart wanting his trust for the last time. "I'm so damned tired of trying to convince you, I no longer care what you think."

Chapter Fourteen

Telling Anton that she no longer cared what he thought and believing it were two completely different things, Hillary learned in the weeks that followed.

Assuring the university's attorney that she would honor their unwritten agreement by not fighting termination of her contract, and accepting that she would no longer face the daily challenge of bright, talented young students, were two others.

Fending off the few persistent, none-too-tactful reporters, and sitting silently while the brief flurry of tabloid interest dissected her attitude, talent and morals, were still two more.

If Anton didn't trust her, he couldn't love her, and she was better off without him, wasn't she? she asked. Right, she answered.

If she didn't have the daily pressure of her teaching duties, she would have more time for her own music, wouldn't she? Right again, she swore.

And no one, absolutely no one, believed what was printed in those newspapers, so nothing they said about her could hurt, could it? Oh, yes, Hillary, she told herself, you are absolutely right.

It was weeks before she asked herself the one question she couldn't answer: if none of those things mattered, why did she hurt so much?

Elaine descended on her early in November, in a swirl of furs, silks and French perfume. Her excuse was that a former client of hers had asked her to fill a temporary assignment as a trust consultant for his bank. Hillary suspected the real reason for her visit was concern for her.

Elaine never pushed her. On the occasions Elaine suggested she join her for an evening out, Hillary always declined, telling her she preferred to stay home and work on her music.

Tippy, after his and Constance's initial, embarrassed visit to apologize to her, was not so gentle. "What music?" he demanded to know, waving sheets of staff paper at her. "There's not one new note on this thing, Hillary. What are you doing to yourself?"

Even Mike Whalen, Tippy's producer, was drawn into the conspiracy. "I know you won't go back on the road," he said in an unexpected telephone call. "I wouldn't even ask you. But I've signed a new girl; she's going to be great—wonderful voice—and I can't find her any decent material. Your kind of stuff would be perfect for her. Don't say no! Not right away. Just let me send you one of her tapes."

Hillary tried to write. She pulled out all the music she had written before. She even seated herself at the piano day after day. When the thought first picked at her mind, she pushed it away. It returned, stronger each time, until she had to admit it. It was as though the outpouring at the church had drained her. For the first time in her life, Hillary had no music.

SHE AND ELAINE WERE SEATED at the breakfast booth in Hillary's cheerful yellow kitchen, lingering over coffee. Hillary found that she did that a lot, lately. Elaine was hidden behind the Sunday paper. Hillary never knew what caused it. Lethargy had become almost a way of life for her, but she wasn't feeling particularly sorry for herself. She began thinking of all she had lost—love, her career, her privacy and now even her creativity, all because of a series of events that had been started by someone else and had careened out of control.

"It isn't fair," she whispered.

Elaine lowered the newspaper to the table.

"It isn't fair," Hillary repeated. "It isn't fair! And I'm not going to let my life be ruined because of it."

Elaine quirked one delicately arched brow as a smile lifted her perfectly sculpted mouth. "It's about time you reached that decision."

STARTING OVER WASN'T SO BAD, Hillary told herself a few weeks later. In fact, she was getting to be quite good at it. It was that awful time when you didn't know where or how to start that she swore she'd never face again.

Mike's new client had been her focus in this beginning. Mike was right. The young woman did have a wonderful voice, and a style that challenged Hillary's imagination. She had already completed two songs for her and was making plans with Mike for an album.

She had also accepted a few of Elaine's invitations and had actually enjoyed being with Elaine's friends.

And she had come to grips with who she was—Hillary Michaels, once known as Rhee Weston, competent singer, writer of songs, aspiring serious musician, who had nothing—well, almost nothing—to be ashamed of.

Her life was just fine; good, in fact, and getting better. Wasn't that right, Hillary? she asked. Oh, yes, she answered, that's right, so very right, except...

Except for a pair of midnight-blue eyes that haunted her dreams. Except for strong arms that would never again hold her. Except for the aching emptiness inside her that nothing—not friends, not family, not even music—could fill.

HILLARY WAS PERCHED on top of her two-step ladder in the closet in an unused guest room, reaching for a box of Christmas ornaments that just barely eluded her fingertips, when the doorbell rang. She hopped, reaching once more for the box before muttering at it and running to answer the door.

Tippy swept her up in a hug, swinging her around. "Merry Christmas," he said as he planted a loud kiss on her mouth.

His laughter was infectious. "You idiot," she chided him. "Put me down."

He did. "You look terrific," he said.

She grinned at him. "You look pretty terrific yourself." She turned to Constance, hugging her carefully, "But you—you look radiant."

That night Hillary and Elaine served their traditional Christmas dinner, although it was two days early, and the four of them decorated the tree after Tippy retrieved the ornaments from the top shelf of the closet. Later they exchanged gifts and showered presents on Constance, whose birthday had been the week before.

"I was a little jealous at first," Elaine told Tippy as they all sat companionably in front of the fire, "thinking of you spending Christmas Day with someone else. But now..." She smiled at Constance. "Now I realize how silly I was. We're together. That's what matters."

"Thank you, Elaine," Constance said softly. "I only hope my family feels the same way."

"They will," Hillary promised her.

"It was Anton's idea," Constance said. "Oh, Lord, they're all going to be there. Ben and Timothy and their wives, and all the cousins. The house is going to be full of people."

"Your family," Hillary reminded her. "People who love you."

"Yes," Constance said, as a smile erased the tension from her face, "they do, don't they?"

ELAINE AND HILLARY spent a quiet Christmas Day together in front of a cheerful fire, with carols playing on the stereo. Elaine seemed lost in her thoughts. Hillary tried her best to avoid hers, especially thoughts of the festivities in the house near Altus. But it did no good. Finally she gave in to them, imagining the aromas floating from Inez's kitchen, the chaos caused by the excited children, the tree in the high-ceilinged living room decorated with ornaments handed down from generation to generation. Anton.

The ringing telephone was a welcome interruption. Hillary hurried to answer it.

"Hillary?" It was Constance, laughing and crying. "Oh, Hillary!"

"What is it? What's wrong?"

"Nothing. Nothing is wrong. Anton told me—he and Mom told me about my mother, about Florence. You were right, Hillary. I did need to know."

She was right? How could Constance have known that? Unless Anton had . . .

"Hillary? Are you still there?"

"Yes." She forced herself to concentrate on this conversation. "How are . . . how are things going?"

"Wonderful. At least now. It was a little bit strained at first." She laughed. "My cousin Carla fainted when she met Tippy, fell flat on her face, and that pretty much broke the tension. It's going...it's...it's better than I ever hoped it would be. I'm just sorry you can't be here with us."

"Oh...well..."

"No, please let me say it. I didn't realize until today what I did to you. Mom told me what you said when you left. Mom told me a lot of things that if I hadn't been so wrapped up in myself I would have seen. You told me it was over between you and Anton. You didn't mean it, Hillary, did you? Because he doesn't blame you for what happened. Not now."

"Connie..." Hillary blinked back a quick mist of tears. "You're there to enjoy Christmas with your family. Please don't worry about me or what you think could have been. When I told you that anything Anton and I might have had was over, I meant it. I still do."

"Hillary." Tippy's voice came over the line, challenging her. "I never thought I'd say it, but he is a pretty decent person."

"I agree," she told him, "but so am I, Tippy." She had to end this conversation, and end it quickly. She motioned for Elaine to come to the telephone. "Your mother wants to talk to you."

HILLARY STOOD AT THE FIREPLACE gazing into the flames. So Anton didn't blame her now. How generous of him, she thought bitterly. How truly generous.

Elaine joined her at the fireplace. Hillary noticed a suspicious moisture in the older woman's eyes. Elaine smiled at her. "It's nothing serious," she said. "I just miss having them with us."

"You told them you wouldn't mind," Hillary said gently.

"Well," Elaine straightened and managed a valiant grin. "I lied. Now," Elaine said, "it's your time for confessions. What put the tears in *your* eyes? It's not because of your father, is it?"

Hillary put her fingers to her cheeks and brushed at the moisture she found there.

"No. I got the usual card—and check. I didn't expect more."

She rested her head against the gaily decorated mantel. Elaine would understand. She always understood. "How much time do you have?" she asked shakily.

She felt Elaine's hand on her shoulder and turned to her. Elaine enfolded her in a comforting hug. "As much as you need," she said.

Elaine listened, commenting only with gentle prompting, while Hillary told her everything, from her initial deception to her last bitter words. They had moved to the sofa, and Hillary sat with her feet tucked beneath her and her head thrown back against the cushions.

"But of course you do still care what he thinks," Elaine said gently.

"Yes."

"And you do still love him."

"Do I, Elaine?" Hillary asked. "I sometimes wonder if I loved *him* at all, if what I loved was the illusion of what I thought he was. He was so ... changed this time ... so withdrawn, so ..."

"Cold?" Elaine asked.

"No, not cold. Seething, maybe; definitely not cold. But he was so different from the way I remembered him. The strength was still there. He took responsibility for everything, from running the vineyard and winery to protecting his mother and Constance. But the softness, the ability to laugh at himself, the ... He doesn't laugh anymore, Elaine. It's as though that's been burned out of him."

Elaine put her hand over Hillary's. "It doesn't sound as though either of you had very much to laugh about."

"No," Hillary admitted, "we didn't."

"And he did tell you he wanted to love you."

"Wanting isn't enough for me," Hillary said. "Not anymore. Not when I know he can never trust me. I hurt him, I know that. He'll never forgive me. I'll never forgive myself."

"Maybe you should," Elaine said. "Maybe that's the only way you'll ever find out if he can."

THE LETTER CAME three days after Christmas, from Constance, on Tippy's heavy, embossed stationery. A folded paper fell from the letter as Hillary opened it.

Constance wrote as she spoke, nonstop, brutally blunt about some things and maddeningly vague about others. "I once thought Anton was the most stubborn person in the world, but you are right up there with him. He loves you. You love him, and don't you dare deny it again. I'm a little embarrassed by the matchmaking I tried on the two of you before I knew what you had meant to each other, but I won't apologize for it. I thought then that you two would be perfect for each other. I still think it. But this isn't matchmaking. It's my way of making up to you for all the misery I put you through. And it's my way of making sure that the two of you can't lock yourself away in your stubborn pride and wounded dignity and refuse even to talk.

"It's because of you that I can do this, that I know I actually have the right.

"You can't return it to me, and it won't do any good to just tear it up. I made sure of that. It's already legally yours no matter what you do with the papers.

"Anton doesn't know. I didn't tell anyone but Tippy and the lawyer. And now you.

"You're already tied to him, Hillary, whether you admit it or not, and he is to you. This doesn't create the tie. It just strengthens it."

With a sense of dread, Hillary bent and picked up the paper that had fallen to the floor.

"Oh, Connie," she moaned.

It was a deed, and without knowing anything about the words and numbers that described the land, Hillary knew it was for Constance's share of the vineyard and winery.

I once thought the only thing he really loved was

this land. Hillary remembered Constance's words. How could she ever forget them? *He's worked his whole life for this place. He kept putting the money back in and he kept putting himself in. It was almost as if he were driven.*

"Oh, Connie," Hillary whispered, "what have you done? He'll never forgive me for this." Hillary clasped her hand to her mouth to keep the words, to keep the sobs from spilling out. There was so much he would never forgive, but this . . .

IT TOOK TWO DAYS and Elaine's help to make the arrangements. Elaine walked with her when Hillary carried her small suitcase to her car. "Are you sure you don't want me to go with you?" she asked again.

"I'm sure," Hillary told her. "I don't know when I'll be back, or even where I'll go after I see him." She caught Elaine in a fierce hug. "Thank you."

FIVE HOURS IN THE CAR. Five hours of interstate highway travel, with nothing to do but think. As if she hadn't been doing enough of that already. Five hours to prepare herself, to plan what she would say to him. Five hours in which her concentration was focused only on Anton. During those five hours, Hillary finally absorbed the truth of Elaine's words: *Maybe you should forgive yourself.*

Inez met her at the door, almost as though she had been waiting for her. "He's leaving, Hillary," she said as she dragged her into her arms, welcoming her. "Another few minutes and you would have missed him."

"Where is he?"

"He went into the fields. I think . . . Do you remember where the Chardonnay is planted?"

Hillary nodded.

"I think you'll find him near there."

NO, ANTON THOUGHT, not even the vineyards brought him peace now. He stood at the northern edge, among the vines that he had once staked his future on, that had brought him still more awards in the judging that year.

In the distance a tractor droned, beginning the work of clearing the land that Bill had finally sold him before leaving to find a place with more excitement, more opportunity. Anton wouldn't miss him.

But it wasn't the thought of Bill, or even of the new land, that had brought him here.

Hillary. Christmas had shown him how wrong he had been about Constance and Tippy; had driven home what Hillary had tried so hard to tell him; and had made him acknowledge, at least to himself, what he had been trying to deny since she had come back into his life.

She lied once. Once, he told himself. Bruised and frightened and running, she had lied to him. And he had taken that lie, built on it, amplified it, embellished it until it colored his thoughts about everything she said or did.

I'm so damned tired of trying to convince you. She

had tried. He couldn't deny that any longer. He couldn't deny her courage in exposing her pride, her feelings, her heart to him any longer, either. And what had he done? He had hidden behind his own pride and demanded still more proof before he'd risk being hurt again.

I no longer care what you think. Had she meant it? He would never know unless he went to her. Now. He only hoped it wasn't already too late. Somehow, he would convince her that he did love her, that he was no longer afraid of loving her.

He saw dust rising from the road winding through the vineyard and resented the intrusion, until the car drew close enough for him to recognize Hillary's Buick. For a fleeting moment he wondered if he had materialized her, if his own thoughts and needs had brought her to him.

He watched as she parked near his car, stepped from hers, and looked across the fields until she saw him. She straightened her shoulders and walked, slim and unyielding, toward him.

HILLARY SAW HIS SOLITARY FIGURE outlined against the vines. Ramrod-straight, Anton revealed nothing of what he thought as Hillary approached. She stopped in front of him.

"Inez said you were leaving. I won't detain you long."

She released her grip on the envelope she carried and held it out to him. "I didn't have anything to do with this."

She saw his puzzled frown as he opened the envelope and took out the deeds—Constance's to her, and the one Hillary had signed returning the land to him.

He folded the deeds and returned them to the envelope. He looked at her, waiting, she knew, for an explanation.

"Please don't be angry with Constance," she said. "She thought it would bring us together. She thought it was a way to force us at least to talk. But I can't keep it, Anton."

"Would you have come if Constance hadn't given you the land?"

"No."

"Would you have ever come back to me, Hillary?"

She looked away from him. *Damn him! And damn the questions in his eyes!* What more did he want from her?

"No." She stared across the fields without seeing them. Her carefully prepared speech mocked her and then refused to be said. "I loved you," she told him. "I think I always will. I know now that you can never love me. I wanted you to. Oh, how I wanted you to love me. But I've accepted that it can never happen."

"I do love you, Hillary."

She turned to him, fighting the turbulent rush of emotions that threatened to shatter her. "But you don't trust me," she said sadly. "That's something I'd always be aware of, that I'd always have to guard against. I'd always have to wonder when your lack of trust would be greater than what you think of as love. I'm not strong enough to do that, Anton.''

She did find the strength to smile at him. ''I won't keep you any longer,'' she said. ''I know you have things to do.'' Oh, Lord, she couldn't cry now, not now! ''Take care of yourself,'' she whispered as she turned and started toward her car.

''Hillary!'' His hoarse cry stopped her. ''I don't have to leave. Not now.''

''I'm going, Anton,'' she said, not looking back at him. ''There's no reason for you not to.''

''I was coming to see you.''

His words seared through her, and she felt her heart catch before beginning an erratic pounding. ''No,'' she whispered.

''To convince you that I do love you.''

''No.'' The word was a whimper.

''That I do trust you.''

Defeated. Defeated by words she had prayed to hear, by the traitorous longings of her body, by the wild hope that surged within her, even though her mind denied them all, she stood desolately alone and unable to take another step away from him.

''Turn around! For God's sake, Hillary, turn around. Please.''

She couldn't refuse the plea in his ragged voice. Slowly she turned to him. He took the few steps separating them and grasped her by the shoulders, crushing the forgotten envelope as he held her.

''Is this what you went through,'' he asked,

"this agony of not being heard, of not being believed?"

She closed her eyes, not wanting to remember what his words too vividly recalled.

He released her. "It's a wonder you don't hate me," he said in a low voice.

She shook her head in mute denial.

"What in God's name do I have to do to prove to you that I do trust you, Hillary? Tell me. I'll do it."

She let herself look at him. He meant it. The truth shone from his eyes. *He really meant it.* "Oh, Anton," she said, "you don't have to do anything."

Her soft words stilled him. He reached to touch her. The envelope dropped from his hand. "I think I do," he said gently.

He bent down and retrieved the envelope. He opened it and took out the two deeds. He only glanced at them. Looking at her, holding her prisoner with the love she now saw in his eyes, he tore one in half, folded it, and tore it again, and again, and again. He tossed the pieces to the ground and handed her the other one.

"Constance wanted it this way," he said softly. "For a child, she can be a very wise woman. Her share of the land is yours now. I'm yours, if you'll have me."

If she would have him?

"Oh, yes," Hillary whispered.

When he reached for her, she went willingly into his arms. This was her home, the only place she ever wanted to be. She turned her face to his and met his kiss, hungry for the love they had to share, that she knew now they would always share.

They stood locked together, oblivious of anything but each other, while a light breeze moved through the vineyard, rustling the leaves still on the vines and scattering the shredded papers at their feet.

You're invited to accept 4 books and a surprise gift Free!

Acceptance Card

Mail to: Harlequin Reader Service®

In the U.S.	In Canada
2504 West Southern Ave.	P.O. Box 2800, Postal Station A
Tempe, AZ 85282	5170 Yonge Street
	Willowdale, Ontario M2N 6J3

YES! Please send me 4 free Harlequin American Romance® novels and my free surprise gift. Then send me 4 brand new novels as they come off the presses. Bill me at the low price of $2.25 each —an 11% saving off the retail price. There are no shipping, handling or other hidden costs. There is no minimum number of books I must purchase. I can always return a shipment and cancel at any time. Even if I never buy another book from Harlequin, the 4 free novels and the surprise gift are mine to keep forever.

154 BPA-BPGE

Name _____ (PLEASE PRINT)

Address _____ Apt. No.

City _____ State/Prov. _____ Zip/Postal Code

This offer is limited to one order per household and not valid to present subscribers. Price is subject to change.　　ACAR-SUB-1